When Geminis Fall

Eoin O'Donovan

When Geminis Fall

Published by Eoin O'Donovan

© Eoin O'Donovan 2020

ISBN 978-1-78222-777-9

Printed in Ireland by Lettertec

One

Staten Island
2.59 am. 9/11/2001

Ross Kingsley glanced down at his watch, the two white gold plated hands telling him it was almost 3 am, and for the fourth consecutive night he would be arriving home at a questionable hour. Knowing his wife Rebecca would be waiting for him to arrive, he wasn't looking forward to the inevitable hostile reception that would greet him once he entered the house.

He anticipated there would be the usual question and answer role-play exercise, the tit for tat rant that could go on for over an hour, especially when she was drinking. If the past couple of months was anything to go by, it was guaranteed that Rebecca would be at least three sheets to the wind and out of control.

'Well here goes,' whispered Ross under his breath, as he pointed the remote controlled zapper in the direction of the black metal gates which appeared at the far end of Hylan Boulevard, an affluent area which nestled on the wealthy leafy fringes of Oakwood, Staten Island.

The big gates opened effortlessly and Ross proceeded to accelerate past them, scattering the white and coffee coloured gravel in all directions as he skillfully manoeuvred the 3 litre turbo diesel machine up the winding driveway, up towards the large red bricked house that stood majestically on the hill in the distance.

At this early hour, most New Yorkers would still be in their beds asleep, alarm clocks set to wake them over the next couple of hours, forcing them from their beds to meet and greet another September morning. But for Ross Kingsley and the people of New York city, today would not be just another dawn awakening from its peaceful slumber, it would be a day that would carve out his destiny, a day that would trigger catastrophic events which would impact on his life, his family and the lives of millions of Americans forever. Although he knew Rebecca would be waiting up for him, itching to hurl questions and accusations, angrily remonstrating her displeasure as to his whereabouts over the past twenty four hours, it no longer mattered.

But for what it was worth, Ross didn't care, he hadn't cared for a while now, particularly the last two years where his wife's dependency on alcohol could no longer be hidden or kept under wraps. Her binge drinking and intolerant behaviour was now becoming an embarrassment, not just to him and his family, but also to the staff of the communications company that he had built over the last five years. The last thing he wanted was the companies reputation to suffer because of her alcohol induced behaviour. For the past couple of years, Rebecca had become immersed in slowly drinking herself into a state of oblivion and was now in the clutches of a bottle of Jack on a daily basis.

Every so often, Rebecca would pledge to give up drinking, seek professional help and join an AA program. The problem was, every time she said it, she had a glass in her hand and it was always going to be tomorrow.

Over a period of time, Jack had become her everyday soul mate, her closest companion and Ross knew this wasn't going to change any time soon.

His company had started out as a small electronics operation serving the people of New York and the surrounding states but Ross was smart and a quick learner, and through sheer hard work and a little bit of luck, the company had grown and expanded beyond his wildest dreams. The company was now regarded as one of the most advanced telecommunication companies in the United States, if not the world, securing lucrative government military contracts along the way. His success was not going unnoticed, and soon he was moving in political circles, shaking hands and rubbing palms with various Governors and senators scattered across the United States.

For Ross, life was completely different. He was riding on the crest of a wave, the business was growing bigger and better as each year went by, endorsed by the fact that chief executives of some of the largest and most advanced Intel security corporations in the US had voted him businessman of the year for the past two years. In some circles, particularly in Washington, it was rumoured that he was being considered as the democratic nomination of Governor of New York for the next campaign, which if successful, would eventually create a path to the Oval office. As far as he was concerned, he couldn't receive a higher endorsement than that.

His personal life had also changed for the better, especially since that evening in Washington, D. C. last July. He had been invited as the main guest speaker at a college sponsored graduate function when he first set eyes on the delectable Ms. Johnson.

Eve Johnson was exquisite, a stunningly tall and beautiful brunette, she could illuminate a darkened room with her youthful beauty and charm, which was complimented by a robust and lustful passion for life. From the moment he saw her, he was besotted, infatuated by her beauty and her elegance. In his eyes, she possessed everything in a woman that he could have ever dreamed of, and he wanted and craved her so badly.

Ross had gone out of his way to be introduced to Eve that evening and they hit it off immediately. She had managed to stir something inside him, something that he could not, or would not let go of, and by the time they had begun their affair, she had completely and overwhelmingly consumed him.

He had fallen totally in love with this beautiful woman, lavishing her with luxurious gifts such as diamond necklace's, gold earrings, the best that money could buy, while all he could think of was being with her wherever and whenever he could.

To achieve this, he knew he would have to get rid of Rebecca for good, he wanted her out of his life permanently and at this point in time it didn't matter how he did it, he just knew it had to be done and if it caused pain and suffering to anybody who got in his way, then so be it.

However, Ross had to be careful how he went about this, so as not to raise suspicion on himself. He had already spoken to an ex marine who would get rid of his problem, make her death look like an accident if the price was right. Ross refused to pay the asking price, telling the ex marine it was too high. Ross figured that the guy would come back eventually with a lower price offer to complete the job.

Over the past couple of years, Ross had amassed a huge fortune from his Intel communications company which he aptly named ame**RK**omm. He liked the idea that the bold RK lettering in the company name bore his initials, symbolising what he believed was a statement to the world that he owned and controlled the company. Unfortunately for Ross, this was not the case. Although he considered himself the driving force behind the operation, the R in ame**RK**omm did not just stand for Ross, it also stood for the other major partner in the company, his wife Rebecca. When the company was set up in 1996, a large percentage of the initial start up cost came from his father in law's wealth.

Rebecca's father Bob was an industrialist, a hugely successful steel magnate who owned a couple of large smelting foundries spread across the states of Michigan and Indiana. Bob readily handed over the money required, in return for a ten percent shareholding investment in the company.

As part of the initial start up contract, Bob had stipulated that his daughter Rebecca should become an equal partner in the business, which to Ross, at the time, seemed a reasonable request.

Rebecca however, being the bitch that she was, also asked Daddy to stipulate in the contract that if she and Ross ever separated or divorced, twenty five percent of Ross's shares, regardless of their value, would be transferred to her shareholding, which at seventy percent would make her the prime shareholder of the company. Ross had no option but to agree to this, he knew that without her father's financial backing, the business would never get off the ground and his gut instinct told him to go along with it, at least for now. The most important thing was to get the old man on board to kick-start the business, he would address the contract issue's when the opportunity arose sometime in the future.

Ross now knew what he had to do, there was only one way out of this nightmare and it had reached the point where Rebecca had to be taken out of the existing situation. More importantly, with his wife out of the loop, it would also mean that he would become the major shareholder of the company. The initial contract had also stipulated, that in the event of the demise of either partner, their shares would automatically transfer over to the remaining spouse. This meant that with Rebecca out of the way, Ross would own ninety percent of the company's shares, giving him almost full control of the multi million dollar company, something that he had always dreamed of. He knew the time was fast approaching when he would have to act in order to realise those dreams and it would have to be sooner rather than later if they were to become reality.

As the sedan screeched to a halt at the front of the house, Ross exited the car and quickly proceeded to jump the steps leading up to the house, two at a time.

He quietly entered the house through the main doors, checking that the alarm was off, and in almost total darkness, navigated his way up the winding stairs towards Rebecca's bedroom on the first floor. They hadn't slept in the same bed for almost three years, his decision, not hers, and as he silently climbed the winding stairs, step by step, he could smell the strong, sometimes overpowering lilac fragrances that passed through his nostrils, the fragrances that could only come from those burning incense sticks Rebecca would conveniently place around the house, especially when she was in one of her foul moods, only this time the odours were coming from the direction of the bathroom. On reaching the top of the stairs, Ross saw that the lights in the bathroom were dimmed down low and he silently made his way towards the bathroom door.

Rebecca would put on these performances when she was in one of her moods, when she was feeling down, and over time she had convinced herself that it was him who was to blame for everything. Ross eased past the door and stepped into the bathroom, his eyes focusing on his pale faced wife who was almost totally submerged in the jacuzzi bathtub, eyes closed, and up to her neck in bubbles and foam, soaking up the rewards of a hard day's drinking.

Unsurprisingly, Rebecca was clutching a whiskey glass in one hand with the half bottle of Jack placed conveniently at the side of the bathtub. He knew from experience that this wasn't good, this wasn't good at all…

Rebecca opened her bloodshot eyes to greet him.

'*Where the fuck have you been all night…?* Wait…, don't tell me, you've been out screwing that little fucking bitch again haven't you? Well *haven't you*…!!?' she yelled. 'You think I don't know what's going on in this town? Well, let me tell you something…, Mr fucking Casanova, I know exactly what's going on, I know you've been parading your little whore around the trendy bars and night clubs in the city, I know who she is, I even know where she lives for fucks sake!!'

Rebecca pushed the bubbly foam away and leaned across the bathtub, slowly tilting the bottle as she filled her glass close to the brim. There was no glass half empty for Rebecca, every glass had to be at least three quarters full. This time, just for good measure, she also took a swig from the bottle before putting it back down in its resting place.

'I have the proof Ross, I have video recordings, audio recordings, close ups and some very, *very* revealing photographs of you and your piece of trash…

I've had you followed, I've had you and your fancy woman under surveillance for the past two months, I know *exactly* what's going on and believe me when I say this Ross, whatever about her, this is the last time that you're going to fucking screw me around, do you hear me? *Do you fucking hear me!!?*

'Oh shut the fuck up, you dumb stupid drunk!' retorted Ross, 'pissed as usual, your brain soaked in alcohol and your mind playing games, mumbling on about crazy stuff that comes into your head. Do you have any idea how many times I tried to ring you tonight!!? You wouldn't answer my calls, your mobile just went to voice mail each time I rang, you're obviously too drunk to even know where it is, never mind answering the fucking thing!'

'If you must know, I don't have my mobile phone with me, I left it in Michelle's office earlier today and hey…, guess what Mr Casanova, guess what I was doing in my sister's office today…?'

Ross stood there and said nothing, but he had a good idea why she was there.

'Go on, have a guess…, come on Ross, you're supposed to be the clever one.'

Rebecca now had a smirk across her face, that smirk she would wear when she was drunk, and he hated that smirk, he hated it more than anything and was doing his best to remain calm.

'Gee Ross, for somebody that's as cunning and devious as you, you surprise me, not like you to be stuck for words, not like you at all…, let me tell you what I was up to with Michelle today, my sister and I were discussing my best options regarding our impending divorce, and how soon she could make it happen.'

Still wearing that annoying smirk, Rebecca told Ross that Michelle had rang on the landline telling her she had left her mobile phone in the office, and should she be anywhere near her office tomorrow, to call in and collect it.

'I suggested to Michelle that I would call in sometime tomorrow morning, where we could discuss further my divorce options and in the process, nail you to the cross! I'm divorcing you Ross…, and by the time Daddy and I are finished with you, you'll be lucky if we give you a job working in the fucking mail room! Let's see how your pretty little whore reacts to that Ross, the fact that you are going to lose almost everything, will she stand by you then? I don't think so, maybe you're not the Casanova that you think you are after all…!!'

Ross was now standing over Rebecca, but continued to remain silent. There was that smirk again, he despised it so much, it had a tendency to push him over the edge and he knew that right now he wasn't far from stepping off that cliff, but he chose to remain calm, evaluate the outcome of the scenario which was playing out before him. If Rebecca got her divorce he was fucked, although he was already a wealthy man on paper, he would end up with just twenty per cent of the company, he would lose millions, her father would make his life hell, he might as well apply for the janitors job, probably end up cleaning out the toilets!

Michelle was Rebecca's twin sister, a renowned divorce lawyer, hugely respected by her peers, she boasted an impressive success rate, obtaining lucrative divorce settlements in favour of her clients who coincidently were all women. Michelle only handled women's divorce cases and up to now had never ended up on the wrong side of a divorce settlement.

Ross had wondered why Michelle was not returning his calls or responding to his emails of late. Over the years, he had gelled pretty well with his sister-in-law and many times had wondered whether he had married the wrong sister. Michelle was a strong attractive individual and she was certainly made of finer steel than her sister, who was now proving to be weak and an embarrassment to the family .

Considering that he was godfather to Michelle's only child Natalie, Ross had always thought that he could rely on her support, but the fact that Eve was now common knowledge, he knew for certain that Michelle would take sides with her sister in any impending divorce case. Ross knew that this was not good news, he had been naive, he had lacked judgement and in hindsight he should have agreed to pay the initial asking price the ex-marine had asked for. This was not good he thought, up to now he had assumed that Rebecca was happy, even comfortable, in her ignorance that as long as she had a glass of whiskey in her hand, as long as Jack continued to caress her fingers, she was content. Instead it was he who had allowed himself become ignorant, almost complacent in his ways, however, he was not prepared to abdicate his position in the company, nor was he in a financial position to do so.

Beads of sweat were now forming and dancing across his forehead, soon they would be travelling down his cheek bones. His heart was beating at an alarming rate, he knew he had to act, and act swiftly!

This was not how he had planned to kill his wife but he had no intention of forfeiting his shares in the company, he was not going to be deprived of everything he had worked for. A silent rage of insanity had now taken over and he began to move ever so slowly, closer to the bathtub.

He calmly seated himself on the edge of the large round bathtub, and with the palms of his hands facing outwards, he pushed the bubbly foam to the sides of the bath and as he did so, Rebecca's feet appeared just above the surface.

Ross looked deeply into his wife's eyes and gave her a smile, then suddenly and without hesitation, he grabbed both of her feet, pulling them viciously towards his chest. The upper part of Rebecca's body quickly submerged below the water line and she found herself gasping for air, and for her life. Rebecca fought like she had never fought before, frantically trying to kick her legs free while using all of her strength to push her upper body back above the water line.

But Ross was strong, incredibly strong, and he held firm, remaining in the same position until they both knew that her struggle was in vain.

The bubbly bath water quickly entered Rebecca's respiratory system, she could sense a loss of consciousness coming over her as the water quickly filled her lungs, consuming whatever precious oxygen that remained until finally, her body went limp and lifeless.

The sweat dripped furiously from Ross's forehead as he slowly eased his wife's body back into the bathtub, just enough so that her head was still submerged below the water line.

Ross sat motionless for a couple of minutes, taking in what had just happened, inhaling the lilac fragrances that for some strange reason, didn't bother him any more.

It was not lost on Ross, that although Rebecca had fought furiously for her life she was still clutching the whiskey glass in her right hand, while the whiskey bottle danced to the sway of the bathwater at the bottom of the tub. How ironic thought Ross, over the past couple of years, Jack had become her closest companion in life, tonight he would be her partner in death...

2

Captain Mike Fuller acknowledges radio contact from the air traffic control tower at Boston's Logan airport. He has been on this route at least twice a week for the past three months, and with almost twenty years of flying experience on his CV, he feels, in fact he knows that he could fly this little baby to L.A. and back again with his eyes closed.

He slowly guides the commercial aircraft forward, taking his position in the queue behind three other aircraft.

A couple of minutes later, Mike Fuller taxies the aircraft onto runway four, where he will await final clearance for take off.

Meanwhile, back in economy class, Ibraheem Salaah sits uneasily in his allocated seat which is closest to the centre aisle. His eyes are closed, his hands are clenched tightly together and his heart is pounding. Ibraheem is reminiscing on the journey that has brought him this far, and his mind wanders back to the night his father had returned from a top secret Al-Qaeda meeting which Osama Bin Laden had also attended...

As an only child, Ibraheem remembers the constant struggle his parents endured throughout their lives, working hard to put food on the table, clothes on their backs, and providing him with an education that would hopefully ensure a higher standard of living, and a better quality of life for their son. But the hardest struggle of all for Ibraheem and his family was the ever present conflict that raged between his people and the oppressors who threatened the future of his country.

The enemy war machine, along with so called democratic governments of the western world were for years invading middle eastern countries and certainly not by a peaceful nature. They had been bombing and killing men, women and children in their quest to control the massive oil reserves across the Arab world. For the past couple of years, Al-Qaeda had fought to rid their country of these oppressors, and over time they had many successes. But although they were seen as successes back home, they were isolated ones, victories which were played down by governments in collusion with their western friendly media sources, and were not enough to highlight to the world exactly what was happening on the ground in the Middle East.

Ibraheem was proud of his ancestral background, was proud of his parents and particularly of his father who he looked up to with pride, and admiration.

His father Koni Salaah had been an Al-Qaeda officer for over ten years, and had a huge influence on the regional Al-Qaeda forces. His father was blessed with an acute wisdom of combat tactical awareness, and who had over the years strategically planned and carried out attacks on enemy base camps which were strewn across the Middle East. It was also widely believed that his father was a senior advisor and strategic planner to none other than Osama Bin Laden himself.

From his early boyhood years, Ibraheem's father began to educate him in all aspects of his religion, his culture and where his eventual future might lie. His father would proudly tell him of successful missions which he had carried out in the name of Allah and his people. Ibraheem would become very excited on hearing of his father's exploits and couldn't wait to grow up and become a fearless soldier who just like his father would pit his wits against the enemy of Allah. As time went by, it was becoming obvious to Koni Salaah that his son was absorbing everything about his country and its constant struggles. He had sat with him through many long nights discussing ways and means on how to rid their country of its enemies.

Ibraheem recalls one night in particular when his father had returned home having been away for a couple of weeks. He remembers how they both sat in silence under a bright star lit sky, every now and again his father interrupting the stillness of the night by stoking the embers of a red hot fire, until his father eventually turned and addressed his son.

He told Ibraheem, that having watched him grow from a young boy into a mature adult, it was now time to introduce him to the regional Al-Qaeda military council. He went on to explain that for the past couple of weeks at a hidden location somewhere in the mountains west of Pakistan, he along with other regional army council members had met with Osama Bin Laden and his top military advisor's.

At the final meeting before they returned to their families, Bin Laden had made it quiet clear that the next military attacks against the enemy would have to be the most potent yet, a surprise attack on American soil that would instil fear, shock and horror into the hearts of the American people. To strike at the heart of the American business and financial sectors, thus bringing the United States economy to its knees.

It could be a number of attacks over a short period of time, two to three days perhaps, or it could involve a number of relentless attacks within minutes or hours of each other, but they would have to be attacks of ingenuity, attacks that would be totally outrageous to what they had done up to now, something that the Americans themselves wouldn't dream up, attacks that would be the most spectacular of them all! Those strikes would be expected to deliver carnage and destruction to the very doorsteps of democracy, they would rip the very heart out of the so called American dream, except this would not be a dream, but the absolute and ultimate nightmare from hell.

It would be the Armageddon of our time!

Having now got his son's full attention, his father told him that after meeting with the four chosen cell leaders for the last time, Bin Laden speaking on behalf of the army council issued orders to these men, telling them they each had six months to devise a ruthless and cunning plan on how to achieve this. He also emphasised to the cell leaders that they were not to discuss their mission with anybody and certainly not to each other in the event of any of them being captured and tortured by the enemy.

Ibraheem looked into his father's eyes and immediately knew that he was one of the four chosen to serve Allah's cause, to deliver the Armageddon to the shores of America. His chest swelled with pride as he watched the tears appear in his father's eyes. They embraced each other without saying a word, no words were needed. Ibraheem knew that this would be his father's last mission and in all probability a mission that his father would not survive!

Ibraheem decided to sleep under the star soaked sky that night, the full moon illuminating the surrounding landscape as a northerly breeze swept past his face and carried on into the wilderness. However, Ibraheem didn't get much sleep that night, in fact he did not sleep at all. He wanted so much to help his father celebrate not just the honour, but also the responsibility that had been bestowed upon him and his family. Throughout the night, Ibraheem prayed to Allah to provide the inspiration needed for his father to fulfil his pledge to Bin Laden.

As the dawning of another day appeared and the hot dancing sun replaced the bright full moon, Ibraheem rose from his man made bed and again sat by his father's side, this time there were no tears of sorrow, only tears of joy.

Ibraheem could not conceal his joyous face or indeed contain his excitement. His father could also see that his son was full of energy and asked.

'Ibraheem, why are you so excited today? I haven't seen you this excited since you were little.'

'Father,' answered Ibraheem, 'I have spent many hours praying to Allah for inspiration, for guidance, I have asked Allah to show me how I can help you succeed with your mission and Allah has truly answered my prayers. I, your son, Ibraheem Salah am going to help and assist you with your mission.'

'No Ibraheem,' replied his father, 'you are not going to get involved in this, you are still young and inexperienced, it is not your time…, when your time comes, you will know it with all your heart, you will feel it running through your veins, we will not discuss this again, do you hear me?'

'But please father...,' interrupted Ibraheem, 'please listen to what I have to say. Allah came and spoke to me during the night and he has gifted me the perfect mission, a mission that cannot fail, a mission that will not dare to fail. Father, although Bin Laden has chosen you, Allah has chosen *me!!*. He has chosen me to assist you with your mission, and together we will succeed!'

Although Ibraheem's father did not want him to get involved, he did however respect and appreciate his son's maturity, a maturity way beyond his years, and he smiled. He now realised that when he looked across at his son, he was looking at himself – only thirty years younger.

As they walked along the narrow dirt road leading to the foot of the mountains, Ibaheem's mother watched after them, unsure exactly how she was feeling and what she was thinking. She knew the day was coming when she would lose her husband to Allah's struggle, but her heart sank low and a single tear ran down her cheek as she now realised that she could be losing her only son as well. She felt sad knowing that the two most important people in her life would soon be dead, but she also felt proud, knowing that they would die courageously fighting Allah's cause and they would be revered as martyrs for all eternity. She knew that the time was quickly approaching when she would be alone, but she would also be free.

As Ibraheem and his father approached an isolated grassy patch near the foot of the mountains, Koni again questioned his son's indisputable excitement and waited for his response.

'Come father,' said Ibraheem, 'let us sit here awhile, and I promise I will explain everything in detail of what is going through my mind.

As a young boy Ibraheem had always been fascinated with aeroplanes and how they worked, he always wondered how these bird like machines were able to raise themselves off the ground at speed and propel themselves majestically into the sky. During his early years in school, Ibraheem took an interest in aerodynamics and aviation fundamentals. He considered himself lucky that the school library contained half a dozen or so books on the history of aviation, the fundamentals of flight, and an in-depth insight into the most common type of commercial aircraft currently overcrowding the skies above his head. He now knew and understood what made these metal birds soar through the air at ridiculously high altitudes.

Because Ibraheem understood the fundamentals of aerodynamics and although he had never actually experienced flying a plane himself, he knew that if he had some flying lessons and actual cockpit awareness, he was confident that he would be able to control and fly an aeroplane on his own. He was also aware that flying, be it a single engine aircraft or a commercial Jet, the concepts and fundamentals of aviation would remain the same: *"Thrust," "Lift," "Weight"* and *"Drag".*

He leaned towards his father's ear and carefully explained what exactly was going through his mind.

3

This was Zach Muller's first day back from his annual summer vacation, he and his family had spent the last two weeks in Disney World, Orlando. They had stayed at one of the Disney Resorts, the Yacht Club, and although it was expensive, it had been worth it. They had visited all the theme parks, sampled a lot of the restaurants cuisine, the evenings spent attending the many glitzy shows throughout the resort. He had chosen the Yacht Club Resort himself, where everything resembled and reminded the guest of the beauty and the tranquility of the deep blue sea. The rooms and sleeping quarters were decorated like the interior berths of a boat, picture frames on the walls, paintings of boats, sailors and colourful oceans.

The last thing Zach wanted to see on vacation was another aeroplane. The vacation had been pure bliss, but now he was back at work and for his sins, he had been allocated what he called the rush hour slot, which was the airport's busiest hour of the day. He was monitoring five flights for that first hour, one flight scheduled for L.A., two flights to Atlanta, followed by two to Chicago.

Zach sipped on his piping hot Americano coffee and as expected, all radio communication with the cockpits of his five scheduled flights was routine, and thirty minutes later all five planes are in the air and on route to their allocated destinations. About fifty five minutes into his shift, Zach realises that he has lost communication with American Airlines Flight 11 and continues to speak into his radio.

'Flight 11, do you read me?' repeating the question on several occasions but Zach's requests are left unanswered, there is only silence from the other end of the radio.

He now begins to worry and can feel the hairs starting to stand on the back of his neck.

Zach Muller is doing his best to remain calm, but he knows that without radio contact, without verbal communication, flight 11 is now a lonely and isolated bird in the sky. As he continues his efforts to reconnect with the cockpit, Zach discovers not only has he lost radio contact, he has lost the aircraft's transponder signal as well! While he tries to figure out and make sense of what is going on, United Airlines Flight 175 has received secondary clearance from the tower.

Captain Mike Fuller taxies the aircraft onto the main runway where he awaits final clearance for take off. Meanwhile American Airlines base commander, Dave Evans takes an urgent telephone call from senior Flight 11 cabin crew member Stacy Newbank. She tells him that Flight 11 has been hijacked, and that there are at least five or six hijackers on board the aircraft. Stacy also informs him that at least one, maybe two hijackers have entered the cockpit of the plane. She thinks that one of the pilots has been injured as she could see blood stains on one of the hijackers who was standing just inside the cockpit door.

'Stacy, have you tried to make contact with the captain?' Dave asks.

'Yes I have, a couple of times but there is no response, it looks like the cockpit door has now been closed from the inside and there are now three hijackers holding hostages along the centre aisle using what looks like box cutters as weapons.'

Dave Evans knows that they are dealing with an emergency situation and tells Stacy to keep calm, reassures her she is doing fine and to stay on the line while he contacts the emergency unit of the Airline.

Dave speaks to Ed Stiller, head of the terrorism unit at the American Airlines' headquarters and informs him of the situation on board Flight 11.

'I have Stacy on the other line if you want to speak to her,' Dave asks.

'No, it's better you stay with her for now, can she confirm one of the hijackers is in the cockpit with the pilots?'

'Yes, according to Stacy, there is at least one hijacker, possibly two inside the cockpit.'

'Flight 11 cockpit, this is Ed Stiller from American Airlines commander base, do you read me, do you copy...?'

The aircraft, now commandeered by Koni Salaah is heading in the direction of New York city. Using the Hudson River as his visual compass, his first priorities on taking control of the aircraft were to switch off both the radio and the transponder. By doing this, he knows that New York Air traffic control would at this early stage, be confused rather than concerned that something was not quite right high above them in the skies. Koni and his son had calculated that if all the hijackings went as smoothly as planned, by the time Air Traffic Control had figured out what exactly was going on, it would already be too late to stop them. By then it would be a fruitless exercise to scramble fighter aircraft such as F16s into the skies to engage in combat. The F16s would have to take off from Otis Air Base, some three hundred miles away and even then with the transponders switched off, the F16 pilots wouldn't even know where to look and the chances of intercepting them were slim, very very slim.

4

As United Airlines flight 175 taxied its way slowly onto the runway, Ibraheem felt a soft hand on his shoulder and in a startled reflex, opened his eyes. He had imagined it was his father's hand, but instead it was Nancy's, an attractive blonde stewardess who was now looking down on him with a smile,

'Sorry to have startled you Mr Salaah, but you need to buckle your seat belt as we are almost ready for take off.'

'Certainly, will do so immediately,' he answered, 'anything in the interest of safety.'

Ibraheem's eyes followed her as she walked up the centre aisle, meticulously checking that all passengers were fastened in safely, all overhead lockers secure before making her way towards the front of the aircraft. Ibraheem's thoughts reflected back on the last ninety minutes, his cell had arrived at the airport at seven am, they had travelled in pairs and passed through several security gates with the minimum of fuss. He had noticed that two of his younger and inexperienced soldiers were showing signs of nerves and as they passed through each gate he stayed close by their side, guiding them through until they had reached the departure lounge.

Not once were they questioned on why they were travelling to their various destinations, nor were the contents of their backpacks examined after they had passed through numerous X Ray machines. Ibraheem was confident that this would be just another routine day for American airport security. He wondered had the other three travelling cells experienced the same relatively easy passage, and his answer would be a definite yes. They had planned to hijack four aircraft, two that were bound for Los Angeles and two that were bound for Washington, D.C. Their targets were the World Trade Center, the White House and the Pentagon. He was now quietly confident that all would go according to plan, and the fact that they had only factored in a fifty percent success rate for the whole mission, this was all the more pleasing.

Sitting in his seat just minutes before take off, Ibraheem realised that his heart was beating furiously, and he could feel the beads of sweat and perspiration dancing across his forehead. He watched as Nancy replaced the phone back on the receiver and buckle up in one of the cabin crew seats located just left of the cockpit area. As the pounding of his heart grew louder and faster he wondered if Nancy was a virgin and if she was, would Allah gift her to him, alongside the other virgins that would be waiting once he had travelled to the other side, his destiny fulfilled.

Flight 175 taxied towards the main runway, then stopped suddenly. Ibraheem felt the lump in his throat tighten, almost suffocating him. Had they been rumbled? Had someone in airport security realised that they had allowed enemy soldiers on board the aircraft? Had his father struck earlier than anticipated and were air traffic control now shutting down the air space over New York, grounding all commercial aircraft in the process? Was that the reason why Nancy had been on the phone to the cockpit just minutes earlier?

Ibraheem began to sweat, started to panic but regained composure just as quickly as the aircraft once again began to move, began to taxi onto the main runway. The aircraft's powerful engines began to turn faster, the noise getting louder and louder before reaching maximum power, forcing the aircraft to thrust forward pushing him back into his seat.

Ibraheem closed his eyes again and began to smile. For all of his young life he had waited and dreamed of this wonderful day, when he and his father would rain a holocaust of fire and brimstone on the western world. Very soon he would be making the short journey into Allah's paradise, surrounded by the promised virgins including the beautiful Nancy. Ibraheem again felt the lump in his throat, his sweaty palms clutching the seat armrests as flight 175 roared down the runway gaining maximum speed.

The aluminium metal bomb left the ground and soared upwards like an eagle into the blue cloudless September sky. Not long now he thought, not long now. In approximately twenty minutes his life would change forever and he couldn't wait, he couldn't fucking wait!

5

Fire fighter Brad Donovan sucked on a lozenge as he hummed along to the tune of one of his favourite songs which was playing on the radio. His hands resting on the steering wheel of his 4 x 4 station wagon, with Brad tapping his fingers to the beat, he was on his way to work and looking forward to a quiet peaceful day. This was what he loved most about the United States, the land of opportunity, the birth place of the Yankee dollar and above all, the land of the free.

Brad was born in Brooklyn but was of Irish decent. His grandfather Mike Donovan had travelled over to the east coast of America from Ireland in the early nineteen hundreds, settling down in Brooklyn where he was employed as a fire engine nozzle guy. A lot of Irish people who had travelled to the United States around that time, either joined the New York police department or the New York fire department. Brad's father Frank, chose his calling to the fire department and had risen to the position of captain and was now not just his father, but his boss as well. He also had two other brothers serving as fire fighters, but on the advice of their father, all three sons had enlisted in different ladder outfits.

Older brother James was based in the Bronx, while younger brother Michael, opted to work in Queens.

Brad understood the logic of his father's reasoning for this. Experience had taught Frank Donovan that you never enlist your kids into the same ladder outfit. It had become something of a tradition for siblings to follow in their father's footsteps, enlisting in the same ladder unit but this was not for Frank Donovan. Over the years, Frank had witnessed fire fighting families perish in situations because siblings had done just that. A couple of years earlier, a close friend and colleague of Frank's, Captain Patrick Redford, a fire officer held in high esteem by many of his peer's, and the recipient of many commendations for bravery, was assisting a call out to a blaze inside a ten story building in the Bronx. Patrick accompanied by his three fire fighting sons had entered the building in an attempt to put out the blaze, which was getting out of control on the fourth and fifth floors. They never came out alive, the old building collapsed and the Redford family perished beneath the rubble. For that reason alone, Frank insisted that his sons would be kept apart whilst serving the good people of New York city.

For Brad, it was just another beautiful morning, a crystal clear September sky, not a cloud to be seen and not a care in the world.

When he had left home thirty minutes earlier, he had kissed his wife Cathy goodbye, stole kisses from the five year old twins as they slept and was now heading into the city to take up his shift in downtown Manhattan.

Seven years earlier Brad had married his childhood sweetheart, whose grandparents had also travelled across from Ireland.

They first met at an Irish social event on the eve of the St Patrick's day parade, agreeing to meet up again the following day where they walked the parade together, laughing and giggling, holding hands for the duration of the parade. From that day onwards they were inseparable and spent as much time together as they possibly could. Brad knew that day he was in love with Cathy and wanted to share the rest of his life with this beautiful amazing woman. One year after they had married, Cathy gave birth to twins John and James. They had both decided that for the first couple of years Cathy would stay at home and look after the boys.

For the past eight years he had been attached to ladder 43 and was following a proud tradition of family influence in the NYFD. Brad reckoned he was the happiest and luckiest guy in the world.

On entering Manhattan, Brad drove past a primary school run by the catholic church.

He had heard good reports about the school and had spoken to Cathy about enrolling the twins for the coming year. That way, depending on his rosters, he could drop the boys to school in the morning on the way to work and meet up with Cathy and the kids after school for the ride home. Either way he thought, it was a win

win situation.

As Brad began to turn the station wagon into the underground car park next to station 43, he caught a glimpse of the low flying aircraft coming from the direction of the Hudson river at an unusual high rate of speed.

Although he found it strange, Brad reckoned that it was part of a military exercise being carried out by the US air force or even the US navy, either way he assumed the pilots in the cockpit knew what they were doing. What Brad Donovan didn't know at the time, was that today his luck was going to change, change in an unimaginable and horrific fashion that would leave him with deeply embedded scars for the rest of his life.

6

Koni Salaah was closing in on New York city, he was approximately fifteen miles out from his target and he could just about make out the skyline of Manhattan.

His heart was pounding like never before. His whole life flashed before him, particularly the last hour or so where with the minimum of fuss and with little or no resistance, he and his cell team had taken control of the aircraft just as they had planned.

Koni knew he had only minutes left, he visualised his wife's smiling face appearing before him. He thanked her for the love, support and devotion she had unselfishly bestowed upon him over the years, but above all else, he thanked her for giving him a son who would make them both proud and who after today would be revered as a martyr to his people.

In fact after today, they would all become martyrs, immortalised throughout the world for all eternity.

As Koni Salaah steered the aircraft high above the Hudson river, he begins to focus on his target. He descends another three thousand feet while increasing speed dramatically. The aircraft computer alarm systems were now going crazy in the cockpit amid warnings of "EXCESS SPEED", "TERRAIN APPROACHING" and "LOW ALTITUDE SENSITIVITY".

His target, the North Tower of the World Trade Center was now only about two miles out and it seemed to grow bigger and taller as each second ticked by. In what was now the last minute of Flight 11's final journey, Koni Salaah resumed his prayers and as the aircraft approached the North Tower at a speed of three hundred and fifty miles per hour, the screams of *'Allah is great! Allah is great! Allah is great!'* could be heard coming from the cockpit.

It was the last voice that any of the passengers would ever hear as the aircraft crashed into the North Tower building, blowing a massive gaping hole between floors seventy five and eighty one, killing hundreds of people instantly while creating a massive inferno that the inhabitants of New York city had never seen or experienced before.

7

At twenty thousand feet, Flight 175 Captain Mike Connors switched to auto pilot, unbuckling his seat belt as he did so. This was the time when he would get up to stretch his legs, take his usual walk through the aircraft, and converse with some of the passengers on board, all part of the airline's company policy.

While Mike Connors was still thinking about his next movements, Ibraheem had already made eye-contact with his men and he was now walking up the centre-aisle towards the cockpit.

Looking around, he observed his men taking up their positions throughout the plane. He tapped on the shoulder of Kameel Kammal who was sitting in row three, close to the cockpit. Kameel immediately rose from his seat and was now alongside Ibraheem as they approached the cockpit door. Nancy, who was in the service galley at the front of the plane preparing refreshments for some of the passengers saw them approaching and asked,

'Can I help you Mr Salaah?'

Ibraheem said nothing as he pushed her aside, and she was grappled to the floor by Kameel. In one swift movement, Ibraheem opened the door and entered the cockpit.

Outside in the aisle way, Mustafa was holding a female passenger hostage, pressing the box cutter blade against her throat, yelling instructions to the other passengers.

'Everybody stay in your seats and you will not get hurt, this is a hijacking … we have taken control of the plane, do not attempt anything stupid or put anybody's life at risk. We will be returning to the airport to begin negotiations for your safe release. Any attempt to disobey my instructions and not alone does this woman die but we will also kill the captain and his co-pilot!'

From here on, having ruthlessly disposed of the captain and co-pilot, Ibraheem knew it was going to be so easy. Ibraheem took up his position in the captain's seat, switched off both the auto pilot and the transponder. He then altered the flight settings, manoeuvred the plane around to travel due south and just like his father had done twenty minutes earlier, he sought out his visual compass, the Hudson River, and piloted the aircraft back towards New York city.

Ibraheem ordered Kameel to leave the cockpit, instructing him to check that all was under control with the other cell members. Immediately after Kameel had left the cockpit, Ibraheem locked the cockpit door from the inside, Ibraheem slumped back into Mike Connors' seat and reflected on what had just happened.

He now had full control of the aircraft and he smiled, he could not believe how easy it had been, he had persuaded everybody that it would be easy but had never imagined or believed that it would be this easy. He prayed that his father had enjoyed the same easy ride that he was now experiencing. Now it was up to him, and hopefully he would successfully follow in his father's footsteps.

As the aircraft flew high over the Hudson river, Ibraheem held a firm grip on the joystick, dramatically increased the speed of Flight 175 and headed back in the direction of New York city.

8

Ross Kingsley woke with a jolt and a throbbing headache, his mobile phone was ringing out on the floor beneath him. With the inside's of his head crashing and thumping furiously, his dry tongue feeling as rough as sandpaper, he reluctantly picked up the phone. The flashing screen told him it was his operations manager George Lucas on the line. Ross was undecided whether to take the call or not, but throughout his professional career, he always believed that answering a phone would somehow create an opportunity of some sort, and so habit made him press the receiver button.

'Good morning George, what's up?' asked Ross as the projecting images of what had happened a couple of hours earlier in the bathroom, flashed rapidly through his confused brain.

'What's up? he asks,' whispered George under his breath, *'Jesus Christ, Ross,'* shouted George, 'why the fuck don't you answer your phone?'

'Calm down George, calm down' Ross said, 'I'm answering it now aren't I? What's got you so worked up this morning, what time is it anyway?'

'WHAT'S GOT ME SO WORKED UP? HAVEN'T YOU SEEN THE NEWS? HAVEN'T YOU HEARD WHAT'S JUST HAPPENED? SWITCH ON YOUR TELEVISION!' George roared at him.

'Sure thing, which channel?'

'Ross, it doesn't matter which channel, it's on *every fucking channel!*'

Ross was a little perplexed by George's outburst, it wasn't like him to exaggerate or get excited over something. Ross picked himself up off the bed, grabbed the remote and switched on the television. He couldn't believe what he was seeing on the fifty inch flat screen and he quickly forgot about his pounding headache. Ross slowly lifted the phone back to his ear as he watched the flames and smoke billowing from the North Tower.

'What the fuck happened?' he asked.

'Not quite sure,' answered George.

'There's speculation that a private twin engine plane may have crashed into the tower.'

Ross paused for a moment, looking at the images on the screen, there was no way this was a small twin engine aircraft, this was a large aircraft, possibly a commercial aeroplane and looking at the devastation it had caused, it was an aircraft with a lot of fuel on board, there was no doubt about that!

'Doesn't Rebecca have a sister working in one of the Towers?' George asked.

'Ross ... are you still with me? ... Ross! ... ROSS!'

'Yeah, yeah I'm still with you, and yes she does,' he answered.

'Her name's Michelle, she's a divorce lawyer, a senior partner with one of the big law firms and a damn good one she is too!' – (*too fucking good at times*) Ross thought to himself – 'But she should be okay, her office is on the eighty fifth floor of the South Tower, but, you know what George, I'm going to call her right now, just to make sure she's okay, Michelle and Rebecca are very close, especially being twins, in fact Rebecca was going to call in to see her sometime this morning. George, I'll catch up with you later at the office.'

Ross hung up and sat on the edge of the bed. He was still trying to make sense of what had happened, but the pounding in his head had not gone away and his brain cells were not functioning very well. He got to his feet and walked towards the bathroom.

On entering, he could still smell the lavender fragrance in the air, he cast his eyes over Rebecca's cold blue body, still submerged in the bathtub water, the bubbles and the foam had long disappeared, the bottle of Jack had found a resting place between her legs, and the whiskey glass was still nestling between her fingers.

Ross walked towards the bathtub placing his hands under Rebecca's arms and locked them together. Pressing his arms against her chest, he dragged her limp body out of the water and onto the cold black tiles. What a pity he thought to himself, what a fucking pity she wasn't in the North Tower earlier, if she had, it would have solved all his problems.

Ross could not believe how calm he was, his wife, who he had murdered just hours earlier was now slumped on the bathroom floor and his heartbeat was as regular as it had ever been. He needed time to figure out how he was going to handle this mess, but the first thing he was going to do was to ring his sister-in- law.

He knew that Rebecca's mobile phone was still in her sister's office, the fact that he was ringing Rebecca's phone would mean that he believed his wife was still alive. There was no time to waste!

9

With lights flashing, and sirens wailing, Ladder 43 was travelling through downtown Manhattan at speeds Brad Donovan had never experienced in the wagon before. This was surely the biggest and most dangerous assignment that he and his team had ever come across. He had only just arrived at the station when the call came in, he didn't even have time for his first mug of coffee of the day. He fiddled nervously with the Joan of Arc medal that hung from a silver chain around his neck, a gift, a token that his Grandmother had given him many years earlier. She had made him promise that he would always wear it, regardless of whether he was fire fighting or otherwise. She always maintained that as long as he wore the medal of the adopted patron saint of France, who herself was burned to the stake in 1641, she would protect him always and never leave his side.

As Ladder 43 roared down Washington Street, the magnitude of what had happened fifteen minutes earlier suddenly struck home with Brad, then and only then, did he fully realise the dangerous and daunting task that lay ahead.

Although they were one of the first ladder's to get the emergency call, Brad was taken aback at the amount of fire trucks and fire fighters already on the scene.

Hundreds of responders were scattered all over the area, taking up vantage points and staging units around the vicinity of the Towers. He knew there would be casualties, hundreds of them, survivors who would need immediate paramedic attention, people with third degree burns, broken limbs and smoke inhalation. However on seeing the devastation up close, Brad realised that the people who were in most danger were the ones that were trapped in the offices and stairwells above the impacted area. With the elevators almost certainly out of service, and the possibility that some of the stairwells were blocked, or had collapsed altogether, there was no alternative route out of the building and people would surely die, either by heat or smoke inhalation from the black smoke clouds billowing inside and outside the building.

But what really puzzled Brad, was how a commercial aircraft could actually crash into the North Tower on such a beautiful morning. He recalled from reading old logbooks, and looking at framed archive photographs back at the station, there had only ever been one aviation incident in and around New York city.

That was back in the nineteen forties, when a B25 aircraft crashed into the Empire State building on a damp and foggy day, yet almost sixty years later a commercial airliner with top of the range computerised aviation technology and without a single cloud in the sky, crashes directly into one of the tallest buildings in the United States.

It just didn't make sense, nowadays planes practically flew themselves and judging by the devastation of the impact, it certainly did not have fuel issues, plus the fact that since the B25 incident, there was a blanket ban on civilian aviation activity within the parameters of New York city, resulting in the city becoming practically a no fly zone, to Brad it just didn't make sense at all.

For now, Brad accepted this was not the time nor the place to question what had happened, this was a time for teamwork where every available player on the Ladder 43 team, would be out there on the baseball ground, pitching and batting for each other. As Ladder 43 approached the North Tower, the magnitude of the carnage and horror was becoming more and more apparent before Brad's eyes. The fire engine screeched to a halt close to the perimeter on Upper West Street. All ten fire fighters, including Brad, ran to the entrance of the North Tower building which was about two hundred meters inside the perimeter.

What horrified him most was watching people jumping to their death from the top floors, preferring to take their own lives rather than suffocating or being burned alive. At one stage Brad watched in disbelief as two people jumped from the 102nd floor, holding hands as they plummeted to their death onto the pavement below. It was almost as dangerous to be outside of the building as it was to be inside. If one of those jumper's fell on anybody at ground level and at that speed, it would surely kill them instantly. Once inside the building, Brad's unit made their way to the temporary command post on the ground floor. They were met by other teams of fire fighters from fire houses across the city, all waiting in the lobby to be briefed by senior officers on how best to tackle the situation.

In the meantime, Brad was checking and double checking that his unit were fully equipped for the job ahead, checking their fire fighting gear, breathing masks, radios, hand torch, axe and compressed air cylinders were all in working order.

He slowly scanned the area, observing all points of exit, stairwells and elevator shafts. Brad stood in line with the other units, waiting, itching for instructions from one of the chiefs. As he did so, every now and again he would hear the thud of bodies hitting the pavements outside, people still jumping to their death from the upper floors of the Tower.

Brad got out his mobile phone and rang his wife at home.

'Hi honey, are you okay?' asked Cathy as she answered his call, 'I just heard it on the news this minute, are you there? Are you at the scene?'

'Yes babe, I'm at the scene, but don't worry, I'm okay, I'm in the lobby of the North Tower as we speak, waiting for instructions.

'Are the kids up yet?'

'Yes they are, they're in the kitchen having breakfast.'

'Do me a favour babe, do not turn on the television until you get a chance to do so on your own. Things are a bit scary down here at the moment, a lot of people are trapped in the upper floors of the Tower and to be honest, their chances of survival are not looking good!

Cathy, I'm watching people who are actually jumping to their death from the top floors of the building.

This is a living hell at the moment, and I don't think we can do a lot to rescue those trapped above the impacted area!

Cathy I've got to go now, give my boy's a big kiss for me. I love you babe, always have!'

'Bradley Donovan,' Cathy shouted down the phone, 'you just make sure you come home to me and the boys tonight, *do you hear me!!?* We need you to make it home tonight!'

Brad never heard the last few lines of the conversation with his wife. By the time Cathy had finished talking, his mobile had been switched off and put back in his pocket.

10

As Ibraheem Salaah guided the aircraft towards New York city, it was still flying at an altitude of twenty thousand feet, high above the Hudson River. He was aware that he would have to descend rapidly and at a crucial speed to ensure that he was directly in line with his target, the South Tower. However because the aircraft would be descending at such speed, he was also aware that if he didn't get it right first time he would not get a second chance and could possibly end up crashing into the Hudson river.

But Ibraheem trusted Allah, he knew that today, Allah would be in the cockpit alongside him to ensure that he would succeed at the first attempt. He could see the black smoke billowing from the North Tower and thanked Allah for his father's success, knowing that *"Little Boy"* had done its job.

Ibraheem recalled how weeks earlier, he and his father had decided to give their hijacked aircraft codenames, they had agreed that the first plane to hit the North Tower would be codenamed *"Little Boy,"* and the second aircraft would be codenamed *"Fat Man"*. These were the code names of the atomic bombs that were dropped on the people of Hiroshima and Nagasaki.

On August 6th 1945, a B-29 aircraft dropped a 9,700 pound nuclear bomb nicknamed *"Little Boy,"*, on the city of Hiroshima, and caused so much havoc, death and destruction, it changed the course of world war two overnight. Three days later, a second nuclear bomb nicknamed *"Fat Man"* would be off-loaded on the city of Nagasaki, from another B-29 aircraft bomber, codenamed "Bockscar", again bringing devastation, suffering and death to the Japanese people. Japan would never recover from this and finally surrendered on August 14th 1945.

If there was ever a case of an existing clear and present danger, this was it, and as Ibraheem pushed the joystick down hard, the nose of the aircraft dipped immediately. Because of the alarming rate of speed that the aircraft was descending, Ibraheem knew that he was taking a huge risk, but thought this was the best option available. It would have been almost twenty minutes since his father's plane had hit the North Tower, they had allowed at most, twenty to thirty minutes before the United States government and its militarized defense system realised that their country was under attack. By the time the United States air force generals gave the order to scramble F16s from the Otis air base, it would be too late. The attacks would have been successful.

11

Michelle Johnson was on her phone speaking to her husband Geoff when Rebecca's mobile started vibrating and sliding across her office desk.

'Hang on Geoff,' she said, 'I think Becky might be trying to get through to me, she was to call to see me some time this morning but considering what's going on, she's probably not going to make it in now, just give me a second sweetheart, won't be long…'

Michelle answered Rebecca's phone and was surprised to hear Ross's voice at the other end of the line.

'Hi Michelle, are you and Rebecca okay?'

'Hello Ross, what can I do for you?' Michelle asked.

'Well I was hoping to talk to Rebecca, I know she's there with you, what's going on down there anyway, what's happened? Are you okay? Is Rebecca okay?'

'Well first of all, Becky hasn't arrived yet, she was due to call this morning to collect her phone, and speak to me on a personal manner but with what's going on here at the moment, I can't see her being allowed anywhere near the building.'

'Where the fuck is she then?' he asked. 'She left the house at around seven this morning, and believe me Michelle, she was in a foul humour, probably the worst I've ever seen her. She was drinking heavily again last night, she got very drunk and now her car is missing. I'm really worried about her state of mind Michelle, I really am…'

Ross hoped that his voice sounded calm and his inquisitive tone was convincing.

'I don't know,' answered Michelle, 'she left her phone in my office yesterday, I spoke to her last night on the house phone and she seemed fine.'

'Okay,' Ross said, 'she obviously hasn't arrived at your place yet, maybe, with what's going on in Manhattan at the moment she saw sense and turned back, she might have decided to stop somewhere for breakfast instead but when she calls you Michelle, tell her to contact me immediately, we have a lot to discuss and hopefully we can resolve our differences and build on our future together.

'Michelle… I suppose you know she's been drinking a lot lately, I'm very concerned about her state of mind.'

'Would you blame her Ross?' asked Michelle, 'she's not very happy with you at the moment, she knows you're with somebody else and believe me, she's determined to do something about it this time. She's finally made up her mind Ross, she's going to divorce you!'

'That's what you fucking think,' thought Ross to himself. He had put contingency plans in place, he had decided earlier that he would drive up to the lake, put his wife's body in the driving seat, conveniently place a quarter bottle of Jack in her jacket pocket before pushing the car into the lake. As she had already been drinking, if and when she was found, the bathtub water would be contaminated with the murky lake water in her lungs. It would appear, because she had been depressed and had been drinking so much, she had decided to end it all. It would be as simple as that, it wasn't what he had planned to happen, but it had and he now had to deal with it and finish the job.

'Look Michelle, I know I have screwed up recently, but believe me, I want to make it right by Rebecca and hopefully she will forgive me and we can move on. Michelle… I do love your sister, you know that, don't you? and I desperately want her back, please help me to win her back Michelle, please…'

Ross bit his lower lip, hoping that he had given a convincing performance, he was confident that he had and switched the conversation.

'What's happening down there?' he asked. 'News bulletins say a light aircraft has crashed into the North Tower, has there been any call to evacuate the South Tower building at all, at least until they know exactly what's going on?'

'Not at the moment,' answered Michelle. 'I contacted security earlier and they say everything is fine, they have assured us there is no need to be alarmed, in fact one of the girls in the office tried to exit the building, to check out what had happened but when she met some security people on the stairwells, she was told to return to her office until further instructions, a bit weird I thought...'

Michelle was not to know, but those words would be the last she would ever speak, with the phone still pressed against her ear, she noticed that the east side of her office had started to darken and she could not understand where the loud screeching noise was coming from.

As she looked up and over to the window, her eyes, just like her mouth had opened fully in disbelief, she wanted to scream, she wanted to scream so badly but the shock and horror of what she was seeing through the office window would not allow it.

For the brief couple of seconds before she died, Michelle Johnson looked at Ibraheem Salaah through the aircraft's cockpit windscreen, she watched as he commanded every sinew, every muscle in his body to steer the aircraft towards her office, towards her imminent death while he chanted *"Allah is great! Allah is great! Allah is great!"*

In that endless fleeting moment, Michelle's voice was silenced, and Rebecca's phone went dead.

12

Just as teams of fire fighters were assembling on the ground floor, ready to begin their climb up the stairwells, a dangerous ascent that would take them to the upper parts of the North Tower, a loud thundering noise reverberated throughout the building, as if a bomb had detonated somewhere on the upper floors of the Tower. Everybody stood still for a couple of moments, trying to take in and understand what was going on.

Brad was one of the first to react and ran towards the main doors of the building. As he stepped outside, he looked up to get a better view of what was going on. His eyes opened wide in disbelief as he looked up and across at the South Tower, Tower number two was now also on fire and just like Tower number one, there was smoke and flames billowing from the upper half of the building.

'HOLY FUCKING SHIT! HOLY FUCKING SHIT! Did you see that!? Did you fucking see that!!?'

'See what?' Brad asked, addressing a civilian office worker who appeared to be in shock, his feet stuck to the ground.

'A second plane just crashed into the South Tower, it just dropped out of the sky man, slammed straight into the building, right in front of my eyes!

'Please tell me this isn't happening man … please tell me this isn't real!'

'Oh it's happening all right and it's real,' Brad muttered, more to himself than to the civilian office worker. His thoughts went back to a little earlier when he questioned how a commercial jet could get it so wrong and crashed directly into a tall building, to happen once would be hard to believe, but was not impossible, but twice in just over twenty minutes was indeed unbelievable and downright impossible. Brad now realised that his country was under attack, and these two strikes were without doubt, acts of terrorism.

On this beautiful September morning, evil forces had declared war on the United States of America and no matter how much history repeatedly tells us to "be prepared", "be armed", the enemy just hit it back in our faces at their leisure. The United States with all its military intelligence, with all its superior armoury and fire power, had just been attacked without response for the second time in twenty minutes.

13

Ross Kingsley slumped backwards onto the couch, watching in disbelief at what was unfolding on the screen in front of him. Although he had never been there, he knew Michelle's office was situated on the eighty fifth floor and instead of being shocked and horrified of what he was witnessing, he crossed his fingers on both hands and started to count the office floors from the top down and began to smile. He couldn't believe his luck, it was the answer to all his problems, marriage, divorce, money, the company, the business, the whole fucking lot. This could very well be the perfect murder he thought to himself, but he needed to act and act fast. He hurried back into the bathroom, immediately casting his eyes on his dead wife's body on the ground, her cold bloodshot eyes looking straight back at him. She hadn't moved an inch, her body was as he had left it a couple of hours earlier.

His brain was now in overdrive, for a moment he had thought about burying her under the grounds of the house but then thought differently. It would be too risky, he couldn't take the chance some pesky inquisitive cop might come calling to the house, sniffing around, looking for clues.

He decided that he would stick with his original plan and take her to the lake, however because the circumstances had changed he had to make sure that her body would never be found ... ever.

He took hold of Rebecca's legs, dragging her stiffening cold body down the stairs, the gold bangle on the wrist of her right hand scratching on each step, making a scraping sound, almost in tandem with the bopping noise of her head as it hit each of the fifteen steps of the stairs until he got to the ground floor.

Ross opened the door to the basement, and using the same drill as before, he hauled Rebecca's body down more steps before reaching the basement. He stopped to catch his breath for a minute before dragging her body across the floor, letting her legs drop in front of the fridge freezer. He was breathing a little heavier again now and could feel his heart was pumping a little faster.

'Must try and get back to the gym,' he thought to himself as he lifted the door of the freezer, the little fridge light coming on as he did so. He was glad and relieved to see the freezer was almost empty.

Other than himself and Rebecca, the only people who had access to the basement were Tom and Julia Hartman. The married couple who were now in their sixties, had been with them for about ten years, Tom looked after the grounds and any odd jobs that needed doing to the house while Julia looked after the housekeeping and was also an excellent cook.

Taking a firm grip on Rebecca's body, he slowly lifted her up over the side of the freezer, dropping her conveniently to the bottom. He covered her body with packs of frozen meat, vegetables, and some bags of ice. Ross closed the freezer door and walked back towards the stairs, the freezer light switching off, leaving Rebecca's body in darkness.

Ross climbed the basement stairs to the kitchen, locking the door behind him, he then sprinted up the stairs to the bathroom, taking his clothes off and stepping into the shower.

As the water cascaded down his back, he showered himself with a body wash, his head still spinning. He pinched himself, asking himself was this really happening, and if it was, he couldn't believe his luck. He quickly dried himself off before dressing smartly just like he always did. The next couple of days would be long and arduous but he didn't care. In the end it would be worth it, he would have everything, he would have it all. Before he left the house, Ross turned to look at the television and for the second time in almost an hour his mouth opened wide, his body frozen as he stared in disbelief, the South Tower was collapsing before his very eyes.

'Holy shit,' he muttered to himself, 'this was unbelievable, this was box-office stuff.' As he walked across the hall, heading for the front door, he stopped and looked in the mirror to check his tie knot was centre, it was something he could never get right, it always tended to move to the left, 'you know what,' he thought to himself, 'today it won't matter, today people won't give a shit whether the knot of his tie is centre or not.' Today he just wanted to be noticed, and he sure as hell knew how he would achieve that. Right now it was time to go to work!

Ross bounded down the steps of the house, activating the central locking in his car as he did so. He opened the door and slid effortlessly into the driver's seat before swiftly accelerating down the driveway, the gates swinging open as he approached the exit that would bring him onto the main street. Watching the metal gates close behind him he pressed the accelerator to the floor and sped back towards the bridge which would take him across the Hudson and into the furnace that was Manhattan. Whilst driving into Manhattan, Ross rang his housekeeper Julia, explaining to her that in view of what was going on, there was no need for her or Tom to turn up for work at the house for the next couple of days. He told her not to worry as they would be paid as usual and that he would get back to her by the weekend to let her know whether he would require their services the following week.

As Ross approached the outskirts of Manhattan, the volume of noise increased with every yard that he travelled. There were fire engines, ambulances, police cars all over the place with sirens wailing, blue and red lights flashing, all heading in the same direction. The streets were covered with white powder, dust particles blowing in the wind, covering cars, buses and trams in what looked like a blanket of snow that had just fallen on Manhattan. About five hundred meters from the Trade Center, Ross was met by a police roadblock manned by two patrol officers. As he drove slowly in the direction of the roadblock, one of the young police officers walked towards his car, the palm of his hand waving frantically in the air indicating to him not to advance any further.

As the cop approached the car, Ross let the window down and stuck his head out of the window,

'Hello Officer' he shouted, 'I need to get through immediately, I need to find my wife, I need to know that she's safe!'

'Sir, I'm afraid you can't do that, you need to turn your car around, a five hundred meter parameter roadblock has been set up around the towers, only police and emergency vehicles are allowed beyond this point, Sir, you gotta turn back!'

'But I need to get through!' shouted Ross as he lapsed into a pretentious fit of hysteria,

'I have to get through, my wife was in the South Tower when the second plane hit, I was speaking to her when her phone went dead. I just need to find her, I need to know that she is okay, please officer, please let me through, please, please let me pass...'

As Ross opened the door and started to get out of his car, the young cop drew his firearm.

'Sir, this is the last time I will ask you to turn your car around and drive away, if not I will have to arrest you and have you taken to the nearest precinct. As you can appreciate, we have more important priorities here today and it will not look good for you before a court judge if you are found in any way to have impeded our efforts to secure the parameter.'

'Okay officer, okay' Ross said, his hands held high above his head. 'I'll get back in my car and turn around, please understand, I just need to know that my wife is safe!'

Dust particles were still falling from the sky and Ross used his screen wash and wiper blades to get a better view as he drove away.

Steering the car in the opposite direction of the roadblock, he looked in the rear view mirror, he could just about make out that the young policeman was writing his car registration number into his notebook.

This pleased Ross as it put him in Manhattan at 9.45am. That went well he thought to himself, feeling pretty pleased with his performance. He then focused his mind on concentrating what was the next best location where he could make a nuisance of himself.

'Got it,' he thought to himself, 'I know just the very place.' and drove off in the direction of one of the jetties on the Hudson river.

14

Brad was speaking to a senior officer of the New York port authority who was outlining the current situation. According to the port official, the information coming through was that the damage to the North Tower was contained from the seventy fourth floor upwards to the ninety second floor. The elevators were out of action and people were making their way safely to the ground floor using the stairwells.

Brad had by then made the decision that he and his team were going in. In a couple of minutes they would be climbing those very same stairwells. Forming a circle, he huddled his team together explaining what he had heard from the port authority official, spelling it out in no uncertain terms what was involved in this massively dangerous rescue operation. Their priority now was to rescue those trapped inside, saving as many lives as possible, even though they would be putting their own lives on the line. He also made it clear to the crew of Ladder 43 that given the circumstances of what was going on around and above them, there was a very real possibility that some of the team themselves might not make it home by the end of the shift.

Brad advised them to ring their loved ones, talk to them, talk to their kids, reassure their families that they would see them again. Even as he spoke, people were gathering above them on the mezzanine floor which circled the lobby. Command chiefs had issued instructions that nobody was to exit the building through the front doors of the Tower, not because of the falling debris, but because of the danger of being hit by jumpers, which were now crashing through the roof just outside the lobby.

After the initial gathering and briefing was over, Brad and his team began their climb, heading for the top floors of the tower. As they cautiously climbed their way up, level by level, they were met by hundreds of people who were now descending from the various floors above. Although it appeared to Brad that there was no organised evacuation plan in place inside the building, he was amazed how calm these people were considering what had just happened, there were no signs whatsoever of panic amongst office employees, visitors or anybody else for that matter, maybe they were still in shock and even if they were, he just couldn't get over how calm and collected they appeared to be as they continued their descent down the stairwells, some even passing bottles of water to the fire fighters, applauding them for their bravery, for their courage in putting their own lives at risk, while attempting to rescue those trapped above them. Making their way slowly upwards, step by step, floor by floor, Brad couldn't help but wonder … was this it? Was this the end of the terrorists' onslaught of attacks.

He was now convinced more than ever that it was a terrorist attack, and wondered what if this was not the full scale of the attacks?, what if there were more strikes on American soil? what would the targets be? the Statue of Liberty, maybe even the President and the White House itself, although he guessed at this stage the President and the white house staff would have been evacuated long before now.

As things stood, no one could predict what was going to happen next, no would could tell for sure. Brad also realised that the aircraft he had seen earlier was not the military plane he had first thought it was, but the actual aircraft that signalled the first strike on the North Tower.

News was now filtering through that a fire fighter had been killed, crushed by a jumper from the North Tower. Brad knew that the present situation didn't look good and as they continued to climb each stairwell, he began to worry about the safety of his crew.

The heat was becoming more intense floor by floor and the smoke was getting thicker, making it harder to breathe.

Some of the radios were not working and he could sense the fear and anxiety on the faces of his crew. He knew that each of his rescue team wore their heart on their sleeve, they knew the risks involved once they were issued with their assignments, but this was one motherfucker of a fire and as they continued to slowly climb upwards, he wondered was he leading them to their death?

He had to make a decision and make it fast! On the sixty seventh floor he called his team together. He made it clear to each one of them that to go any further would be foolish, even suicidal. As far as he was aware, all survivors below the aircraft impacted floors had now gone down through the stairwells to safety. Brad himself was having problems with his own breathing and was struggling to ration his oxygen. He knew his crew were experiencing the same problems and they were becoming weaker as the minutes went by.

As far as he was concerned, it would be insane to proceed any further. The wise move would be to retreat back down the way they came, start assisting the injured on the ground. He reckoned that although they had come this far, it was obvious that there was nothing they could do to save the people trapped on the upper floors of the Tower.

He owed it to his men to keep them alive and lead them back to safety. Even though there were one or two objections from his men, he had made his decision, he gave the command, they were going back down, they were getting out while they could.

Although there was no official evacuation orders given by their superior officers, the crew of Ladder 43 held hands as they descended back down the stairwells, some of them in tears, knowing they were leaving people on the upper floors stranded, helpless, destined to die a horrible death. Brad was aware that without an official evacuation directive, he could be severely disciplined for his action's, but with his radio on the blink and with no contact with the outside world, he convinced himself that he was making the right decision for the safety of his team. In fact, he was more afraid of what his father might think of his decision to evacuate his men from the building, wondering would his father have done the same thing in his position.

As the fire fighters descended to the fifty second floor, the team stopped in their tracks and looked at each other in silence. The

North Tower began to shake and vibrate, and a tremendously loud noise could be heard. After about fifteen seconds, which seemed to last an eternity, the noise and vibration stopped.

Brad was wondering whether another plane had hit the North Tower and ran to a nearby office, hoping to catch a glimpse through the windows.

Looking at the view from an office window, all he could see was white smoke and dust billowing through the air, he couldn't even see the ground below, he then ran to one of the offices on the west side of the building and again could see nothing because of the dust and smoke. It was as if a volcano had erupted in the middle of Manhattan, spewing smoke and white ash into the skies above them. He returned to his crew and they continued their downward descent. On reaching the fifteenth floor, the crew of Ladder 43 took a time-out to rest, whilst also sharing whatever oxygen was left in their tanks.

The crew were just about to continue their journey down to the lobby when the whole building began to shake. Suddenly without warning, this thunderous sound could be heard coming from the floors above them, this massive popping sound, like an anti aircraft gun shooting intermittently. Brad immediately knew what was happening, and shouted at his men to run to the corners of the stairwell and take up crouching positions. He himself raced to the west side of the stairwell, crouched on bended knees, waiting for the floors to come crashing down.

With eyes firmly closed and teeth clenched together, Brad waited as the floors above came crashing down, one on top of the other, making an eerie screeching noise while pressing huge pockets of air downwards as they collapsed to the bottom. Any second now, he thought as he blessed himself with the medal of Joan of Arc, any second now…

During those ten or twelve seconds which seemed to last an eternity, Brad closed his eyes and focused on those precious minutes that he had spent with Cathy and the two boys just a couple of hours earlier.

Since he had joined the fire department he had always hoped and prayed that a day like today would never happen, the day that he would never see or embrace his family again, never to see those beautiful innocent smiles again. A couple of hours earlier he had been deciding on the very first school the kids would go to, thinking how they would grow and mature into fine young men, making their way effortlessly through college and finally contributing to a meaningful society that they had inherited from the generation before them. He had always endeared himself to an old photograph that was stuck to the fridge in the kitchen of their home, held there by a fridge magnet. It showed himself, Cathy and the two boys celebrating their first ever birthday in Central Park.

If he was going to die today, then this was the image that would send him on his way. He opened his eyes and looked at his fellow fire fighters. He wondered had they also found an image that would send them on their way, and he hoped that they had. Brad also realised why the tower had earlier shook violently and why the skies were full of smoke and dust, it was obvious to him now that the South Tower had also collapsed. Brad closed his eyes once more, any second now he thought, any second now and the nightmare would be over...

15

Getting out of Manhattan was now becoming a huge problem for the hundreds of thousands of people fleeing the scene, trying to escape the nightmare that was unfolding behind them. Roads were closed off, the subway systems suspended, or shut down altogether, but there was still one option open, and that was to get people off the island by boat, taking them to safety further down the Hudson River, away from the carnage.

Ross Kingsley parked his car near the end of the road, close to Pier 25. Having walked about twenty meters, he stepped aboard the 960 horse power motor launch that was berthed at the far end of the jetty. The Scorpion's Sting was a luxurious boat, owned by ame**RK**omm for the purpose of wining and dining corporate clients as they cruised up and down the Hudson. The boat could sleep a minimum of eight people and had a top speed of twenty knots per hour. Ross enjoyed being on that boat, particularly the past couple of months where he and Eve had spent some good times and great nights together. He made his way to the bridge, lifted a panel inside the first aid cabinet, and with his fingers, located the ignition key. He started up the engines and piloted the launch up the river towards the piers closest to the World Trade Center.

In a matter of minutes, various independent ferry boats and motor launches were now joining New York police patrol boats, taking people on board, ferrying them further down the Hudson away from the carnage. Some evacuees were soaked in sweat, others soaked in blood and almost all were covered in white dust and debris. Morning had become night as the Devil transformed heaven into hell in just over an hour.

While Ross was turning the boat around to sail up the Hudson river, he heard what he taught were claps of thunder coming from behind and as he turned to look he could not believe what he was seeing, the North Tower was now also disappearing from the skyline, all he could see were huge white clouds of smoke and dust enveloping the landscape of Manhattan, again it looked like a volcano had erupted in the middle of Manhattan, spewing lava and smoke into the air. People were now running for their lives, terrified as the smoke and dust slowly descended, travelling onwards behind them like a ghostly demon chasing down its prey.

There was now a growing exodus of people desperate to get out of New York. Thousands were running frantically towards the ferries that were now berthing at the piers, all hoping to get aboard a ferry that would bring them to safety further down the harbour. Ross docked the "Scorpion Sting" at one of the jetties and began to help people get on board the luxury yacht.

He had to be careful that too many people didn't get on all at once, and flip the boat. One middle aged woman who tried to jostle her way to the front of the queue slipped and fell over the edge into the water. Ross immediately saw the opportunity and seized the moment. Without hesitation he removed his jacket and shoes and dived into the freezing water of the Hudson, grabbing hold of the hysterical woman and with the help of those already on board, managed to get her up onto the boat. Ross was loving this, the hero of the hour, rescuing an old woman from the Hudson River while people begged him to take them on his boat and ferry them to safety.

For a few brief moments, given the enormity of what the last few hours had bestowed upon him, Ross felt more powerful than God himself, he convinced himself, that it was he and not God who decided who would live and who would die. This couldn't get any better, a couple of hours earlier he was deciding how he would dispose of his wife's body, now he was in the full glare of the network's cameras who were recording this live, for the whole world to see.

Even Ross couldn't have realised it at the time, but he was now involved in the biggest evacuation of people in the history of mankind, even Moses, when he parted the Red Sea, allowing his people to flee from Egypt, wouldn't come close to this. It was estimated that in just over ten hours, almost half a million people would be evacuated from the island of Manhattan, and Ross had become one of America's greatest heros. 'America's got a new super hero,' Ross thought to himself, 'and I'm gonna fucking milk this forever!'

16

When Brad brushed the layers of dust from his face and opened his eyes, there was an eerie silence on the eight floor. The thundering force that had rocked the building just seconds before had ceased. It was a surreal moment, he remained in his original position, not sure whether he was able to move or not or maybe he was just too damned afraid to find out. He listened for sounds, for voices, anything that would bring an element of reality to what had just happened. There was debris everywhere, again the air was full of white dust particles, office equipment scattered everywhere, jugged concrete columns that had fallen on their sides, twisted metal, broken glass and the smell of death. The smell of human flesh burning, he had experienced it before, but not to the extent that was now suffocating his lungs.

It was obvious that the remains of those who had perished in the immediate fireball on the upper floors, were now all around him, body parts strewn in all directions after the collapse and he was powerless to do anything. He tried to speak out, to utter some words, to make a noise, a sound that even some of the team would respond to, but he was afraid, he felt like he was in a paralysed state in a parallel place between reality and make believe.

His fear was that if he spoke, it would be returned with silence, it would mean at the very least that he would have lost his men during the avalanche of steel and concrete that had rained down on them just a few minutes earlier. Brad scanned the stairwell looking for signs, for movement, but visibility was not good, he realised that there was only one way to find out if there were other survivors so he began to speak. He called out to his team, to his brothers.

'Hey guys, you okay...? Talk to me guys, tell me you're okay...' but there was no reply, only deafening silence. He switched on his torch light and shone the beam into the nooks and crannies, but there was nothing to be seen. The area where he had stood earlier was entangled with rubble, buckled steel girders and debris, above him there was thousands of tonnes of dead weight pressing down on what was left of the eight floor. He had been cut off from the rest of his crew, unsure of whether they were dead or alive. Even though he already knew the answer, he was not prepared to accept it, he knew the time would come when he would have to, but not right now, not today. He decided the only option open to him was to descend to the ground floor as quickly as possible, before stairwell B collapsed and claimed him as well.

17

10.15 pm. 12/28/2019
(18 years after 9/11)

Ross Kingsley focused his eyes on the restaurant across the other side of the street, he was crouched low in the seat of his car, and with the help of a small pair of binoculars was clearly able to watch Eve and Cliff holding hands, drinking red wine while gazing and smiling into each other's eyes. He had been tempted to go across the street, walk in all guns blazing and beat the crap out of this guy, make an example of this piece of shit that was fucking his wife, fucking her in his house, in his bed. He had been suspicious for a couple of weeks now, ever since that day he arrived home earlier than expected, finding both of them sitting much too close to each other on the couch. Much too close for comfort he thought, Ross had always thought of himself as a quick thinker on his feet so he let it ride, he decided to play a game of wait and see, like a cat and mouse situation, play the patience game, see how it would pan out.

He remembers how Eve looked a little flustered that day, her hair dishevelled, her blouse, with the top three buttons opened, was wrinkled and crumpled as if a raccoon had just rummaged through it.

The guy just sat there calmly, saying nothing as if putting the onus on Eve, relying on her to talk them both out of the situation.

'Oh, hello Darling it's you,' Eve said, endeavouring unsuccessfully to bring a controlled tone to her trembling voice.

'I hadn't expected you back until later this evening, is everything okay?'

'Yeah, everything is fine.' answered Ross,

'The conference finished earlier than expected, so I thought I'd catch an earlier flight home and surprise you.'

Ross turned to the guy sitting on the couch,

'I don't think I have had the pleasure young man' said Ross, extending his hand towards him.

'Oh…, this is eh… Cliff, he's eh..eh.., an interior designer, I've asked him to come over and have a look at the apartment, maybe make a few suggestions about changing the decor, moving the furniture around, stuff like that…' Eve said, the trembling still noticeable in her voice.

'And what do you think Cliff?' Ross asked. 'Do you think the place could do with a facelift?'

'Well darling,' said Eve, 'he hasn't looked over the place yet, in fact Cliff only arrived here at the house just a couple of minutes before you, this is his first time here, so he wouldn't really know.'

Ross walked over to the drinks cabinet and poured himself a bourbon,

'Would you like a drink Cliff?'

'Er…, no thanks Mr Kingsley, too early for me, actually, do you mind if I use the bathroom?'

'Yes of course, it's—' and before Ross could say another word, Cliff had darted towards the downstairs bathroom, which was just beyond the kitchen.

'Is he any good Eve, this guy Cliff?' asked Ross turning to his wife, 'is he up to the job?'

In fact, do we need to decorate the place at all? You know what, tell him that we'll call him if and when we decide to go ahead.'

'Okay, if that's what you want' muttered Eve, as the flushing sound of a cistern in the background faded almost as fast as it had started.

When Cliff returned from the bathroom, Eve told him that they would make a decision in a couple of days and she would get back to him later in the week.

'Have you done some work in any of the other condominiums?' Ross asked.

'You mean this block?' Cliff asked.

'Well, any of the blocks in the area?' queried Ross.

'No I haven't, like I say, it's my first time in this part of town.'

Eve showed Cliff out and returned to the sitting room,

'That was a bit harsh Ross!'

'Yeah maybe it was honey, but I think these guys are only after our money, let's think about it ok, but not right now! Since I'm home earlier than expected, how about we go to the Member's Club tonight, catch up with some of our old friends, we haven't been for awhile so hopefully we haven't been blackballed by our absence.

'Yeah, sounds good' answered Eve, secretly relieved that Ross did not suspect anything. 'I'll go get ready, wont be long darling…'

Ross watched her leave the room, he was deep in thought.

'THE FUCKING BITCH!! THE FUCKING WHORE!!' he was livid, outraged, but he would quell his anger for now.

The events of 9/11 had been good to him, not just because he had got away with murder, but it created a bonanza for his company.

With the security of the United States and its people now uppermost in the minds of the American government, ame**RK**omm had reaped the rewards of combating terrorism. The company's intelligence and satellite communication equipment, plus the production of state of the art weaponry drones ensured that the overflowing well of lucrative Government contracts never dried up. There was no way Ross was going to risk all that, not for that whore and her toy boy.

He would play along with her little game, like a cat plays with a mouse, that's it he thought, time to play cat and mouse, maybe it's even time to check the capacity of the chest freezer up at the old house again!

18

Wendy knows that she must control her fears, she's hoping, that by doing so, she will stay alive, she will survive this ordeal. She estimates that she has been on her own for at least six hours. She is slumped in a wooden chair in the corner of the basement, her limbs beginning to regain some mobility as the minutes tick by. Her wrists are tied, pulled together by nylon tie-wraps which are bound to a solid three inch pipe running down the wall. Wendy scans the basement even though it's dimly lit, the one flickering light on the far wall saves her from being in total darkness.

The basement appears to be an L shaped room, it restricts her from seeing what's around the corner on the opposite side of the wall.

Wendy fears for her life, how could she have been so stupid? How could she have dropped her guard so easily? On her left hand side, there is a small wooden table, on top of it there is a paper plate with what looks like pieces of sausage and bacon, there is also a plastic cup filled with water with a paper straw jutting out of it. Whatever about the food, she is more than glad of the water. Her mouth is dry, her throat is parched and she feels dehydrated. The method in which her hands are bound, means she has to turn her head sideways to eat the food or to drink the water. Wendy manages to adjust her mouth around the straw and gratefully sucks up the cool water which goes some way to help quench her thirst.

Her eyes continue to scan the basement, slowly turning her head from left to right. She can vaguely make out what looks like a collection of wine bottles stored on a wine rack, resting against the far wall, there are some steel buckets, woven baskets and empty apple and orange boxes scattered around the floor. Pushed up against the wall on the far side of the basement, there is a chest freezer, which explains the noise, the humming noise that woke her from her drowsy sleep just minutes earlier.

Although she still feels groggy, Wendy tries to focus on the last few hours to see if she can make sense of what really happened, and what led to the predicament that she now finds herself in.

She recalls that she had arranged to meet her best friend Susan in the "Bootleggers Bar", a trendy "thirty something" bar situated in Queens. It was a ritual that had began over two years ago. Every Friday they would meet up at the bar around six pm, just in time for "Happy Hour".

Both girls, were now in their thirties and single, but not off limits to any handsome good looking guys who might just venture across their path.

Just two professional woman in their own right, enjoying successful careers, no immediate plans of giving up their present lifestyle, not for another couple of years at least.

The bar was beginning to swell with people, which was the norm for a Friday evening. As usual, it was Wendy who arrived first and it wasn't long before she had downed her first Pink Gin. The first one always went down smoothly, especially after a hectic week, but when you're on top of your game and you're selling over a million dollars a week in upmarket real estate, the bonuses you've earned are mounting up by weekend close of business.

Yes, life was good, thought Wendy, reminding herself that it was time for that second gin. She looked up at the clock fixed to the wall above the bar and smiled. It was ten after six and she wondered how Susan always managed to be at least ten minutes late. 'I'll give her the usual fifteen before I give her a call,' she thought.

Susan was a qualified electronics engineer with degrees and diplomas coming out of her ears. She had been acknowledged at an early age, of having a respectably high IQ, sailing through her year's at College with relative ease, finishing in the top three for each of the five years that she attended there.

Susan had been headhunted by numerous companies and for now had settled with working for one of the biggest companies in the world, with manufacturing facilities spanning three continents,

North America, Europe and Asia. It was twelve after six when Ross Kingsley entered the bar, slowly scanning the crowded room. Although it was the second week of January, it was evident that the Christmas spirit was still very much alive, festive decorations hung from the ceiling, the bar itself was still covered in holly and ivy and a Christmas tree which probably needed just one last push for it to fall over, was hidden away in a darkened corner.

Ross continued to scan the diamond shaped bar, looking left to right, top to bottom. This was the perfect opportunity he thought to himself, he knew who he was looking for, the question was would he find her, would she still be there? After about thirty seconds, Ross begins to smile, his concentrated search has paid off, he could see her sitting at the far end of the bar on her own, checking her finger nails. Wendy was a brunette, good looking, and dressed stylishly. Ross admired that in a woman, he liked the way women looked after themselves, the manner in which they fussed after their hair, worried about the complexion and softness of their skin and especially the way they dressed to suit their needs.

Ross had observed that if Wendy had sat three barstools down, she would be sitting right under some mistletoe that still hung from the ceiling. Pity, he thought, he could have used the meaning of Christmas as his opening line. Still, Ross was undeterred, he loved a challenge and was confident that by the time the evening was over, his manly charm would have already seduced her.

Just as Wendy was about to give Susan her fifteen minute reminder, she was interrupted by a smooth, soft toned voice,

'Hi there…, could I interest you in another one of those pink gins?'

Taken by surprise, Wendy looked up and tried hard although unsuccessfully, not to let her jaw drop as fast as it did.

'The name is Ross, Ross Kingsley,' he said as he reached out his hand and made contact with Wendy, who returned the old fashioned handshake mating gesture while smiling shamelessly into his eyes.

'Hi there, I'm Wendy…'

Wendy breaks free from her trance, looking back up to the clock on the wall which now says fourteen minutes past six and for the first time since they had been going to the bar together, she secretly hoped that Susan would not turn up tonight.

'Please don't tell me I'm that boring?' Ross said. 'You're looking up at the clock already…'

'Oh no no!' Wendy blurted out. 'Honestly, its got nothing to do with you, it's just that I'm meeting my friend here this evening, she's usually late, although tonight for some reason she's later than usual.'

'She might be stuck in traffic…' Ross said.

'With Susan, anything is possible, if you don't mind, I'll just give her a call, see what the hell is delaying her, and while I do that, why don't you get me that pink gin that's on offer!'

Wendy barely had the words out of her mouth, when her mobile screen lit up.

'Speak of the devil!' Wendy said, as she put the phone to her ear. 'Hi girl, are you on the way?' she asked.

'Sorry babe, can't make it tonight,' Susan replied. 'Just as I was leaving the office, something important came up and my boss said it had to be sorted before I left for the weekend, this could take a couple of hours, so it looks like I'm not going to make it tonight…'

'Oh, that's okay honey, don't you worry, shit happens, why don't you get your work thing sorted and I'll give you a call tomorrow!'

Susan was somewhat taken aback by the cool response from her friend, she had assumed Wendy would be a little agitated or put out by her not showing up, but no, she seemed to take it in her stride, maybe she was been sarcastic and there was a slight awkward pause between them before Susan spoke again.

'Okay, I'll give you a call sometime tomorrow afternoon and we can catch up, maybe we can organise something for the middle of the week yeah?'

'Of course we will, we'll talk tomorrow,' Wendy said as she started on her second pink gin. Wendy switched off her mobile and slipped it back into her bag.

'Is your friend okay?' Ross asked.

'Yeah she's fine! Something important came up at work that's all, her boss says she can't leave until it's sorted, anyway thanks for the drink, cheers! Can't say I recall seeing you here before Ross, if I did, I probably would have remembered.'

'No, you're right,' Ross replied, sipping on his bourbon. 'Never been here before, and believe me if I had, I certainly would have remembered you!'

'Good answer,' thought Wendy. 'You live around here Ross, or are you just passing through?' asked Wendy as she pushed her seat around to get a full frontal view of the handsome rugged hunk that was standing close to her.

'I live over in Staten Island, just popped over to Queens today to visit an old friend that I hadn't seen for awhile, how about you Wendy, you from around these parts?'

'Yeah, my apartment is just a few blocks down from this joint. Hey Ross, are you married? You got kids?'

'No, I'm not, I'm widowed actually,' Ross replied, knowing that he now had Wendy's full attention. 'My wife died in 2001 when the South Tower was hit and it's taken me a long time to get over her tragic death. It's only recently that I have tried to get my life back on track, so forgive me if I seem a bit out of touch, a bit rusty, this kind of stuff is all new to me again.'

'Wow… I'm sorry, I didn't realise… Christmas must have been pretty tough for you huh…?'

'Yeah, it was tough, but my pain and loss has been gradually easing over the years and I'm sure she… my late wife Rebecca… is glad that I am finally moving on. What about you Wendy?' asked Ross. 'Are you married?'

'Nope, right guy hasn't come along yet!'

'How do you know that the right guy hasn't already slipped through your fingers?'

'Because I'm still happy Ross, I'm still happy!'

'And are you happy now Wendy, are you happy right now?' he asked, as he moved a little closer to her in a totally conspicuous and intimate gesture.

'Well yeah… I guess I am, who wouldn't be happy after a couple of pink gins?'

'So, have you found a new girlfriend yet Ross?' Wendy asked.

'Well I haven't really started looking for one yet, there's no rush… just like you Wendy, there's no rush!'

19

Every so often, the humming noise coming from the freezer would stop, and Wendy could hear the sound of feet scurrying around different parts of the basement but she couldn't see anything. She knew that it could be only one of two things, rats or mice, and she was hoping it would be the latter.

'How the fuck?' she asked herself, 'how the fuck did I end up a prisoner in a basement, tied to a water pipe, secured to a wall?'

She was at a total disadvantage, she was powerless to do anything and it frightened her.

This was not how she had wanted her life to end. She recalled how she had read in some true story magazines about women who had been kidnapped, raped and then killed by their abductors.

She was now starting to struggle with her sanity, a sudden urge came over her to start screaming loudly at the top of her voice but she resisted, she would remain calm, keep her discipline, if only she had kept her discipline last night she thought, she wouldn't be in the situation she now found herself in. She needed to think about her present predicament, try and figure out what was going on and how she could get out of this in one piece. She reckoned that by remaining calm and focused, she would come up with a solution to get her out of the predicament that she was in...

Piece by piece, like a jigsaw, she began to put together the collective thoughts in her mind, she now accepted that more than likely she had been drugged and those drugs whatever they were, were probably still active in her system. Wendy sat back in the wooden chair, composed herself as best she could and tried to join the dots, the dots that would hopefully help her to retrace her steps from the night before. Even though the basement was cold and in almost total darkness, the air was clammy, and did not help with her situation, she was still trying to come to grips with her imprisonment, if indeed, her imprisonment was real. Again, she closed her eyes and focused as much as she could on the night before...

20

'So Ross, what do you do when you're not drinking classic bourbon and chatting up girls?' enquired Wendy.

'Well, first of all I wouldn't mind doing this for a living, sipping a nice bourbon, striking up a conversation with a beautiful and intelligent woman, let me guess, Wendy…, I bet you work in finance, or maybe you're a criminal lawyer with one of the big law firms downtown, have probably been made a partner at this stage, am I right?'

'Maybe you're right and maybe you're wrong Ross, but you still haven't answered my question.'

Ross took another sip from his old fashioned bourbon, and gently placed the glass on a bar napkin while continuing to look Wendy in the eye.

'For now, let's just say I'm in the intelligence gathering business, my company manufactures and supplies the American government with a range of security and Intel products, that's all the information I'm willing to part with at the moment, maybe if I got to know you a little better, I might be a bit more revealing about myself.'

Wendy offered up a cute little smile while she forensically examined the context of what Ross had just said.

'So Wendy, what about you answering my question?'

'What question was that Ross?' she asked, her head bopping slowly to the beat of a piano tune belted out by a balding Billy Joel wannabe who was tucked away in the far corner of the bar.

'The one about you being in finance or sitting at the bar?'

'Well I'm sitting at the bar right now aren't I?' laughed Wendy,

'Ahh … not only is the lady very attractive, but she has a sense of humour as well, definitely not a lawyer then,' laughed Ross.

'Honestly…, I work in real estate, I work for a company that deals exclusively with the high end of the market and believe me when I say high end, I mean up above the clouds where the sky is always blue. I'm talking about the lucrative top layer of the market where the money doesn't matter. People are prepared to pay exorbitant prices to secure the right property in and around New York, particularly Manhattan.

'When I sell an apartment in Manhattan, the buyer is more concerned about the celebrity living next door rather than the actual cost of the property. It's all about the ego's, all about the immaterial things in life, that's what matters to these people.

They don't give a shit about anybody beneath them, they don't care whether the old veteran begging on the street corner makes enough at the end of the day to buy himself a coffee and a sandwich. They're happy as long as their picture pops up on the front page of the gossip magazines, which ironically are bought by people who really can't afford the glossy rags in the first place!'

'Can I give you two a top up?' asked Bill the bartender as he ran a damp cloth across the surface of the bar,

'That depends on the lady' quipped Ross. 'Well what do you say Wendy, one for the road?'

Wendy looked at the clock and then looked back at Ross, it was now approaching eight pm.

'Why not, why the fuck not, one for the road it is, sure who knows, we could be dead tomorrow!!'

'Yes…, that is so true Wendy, that is so true…!'

Wendy didn't see it, but instead of looking up at the clock again, if she had been looking at Ross's facial expression at that precise moment, it was possible that she might have sensed the dangerous predicament she was in, the danger that in the next day or two, she would be dead, very very dead…

21

Slowly but surely, Wendy starts to put the pieces together and in doing so, an ice cold chill runs down her spine, she remembers that just before they left the bar together, Ross had shown her a couple of photos of his mansion on the hill which he had stored on his phone, his Shangri-La as he liked to call it. He had told her that he was considering the idea of moving out of New York altogether, the city was beginning to irritate him, traffic congestion, human congestion, impolite people with their heads constantly stuck in their six inch screens, totally oblivious to the world around them.

'Do you know Wendy…, I took a train over to Queens earlier in the week, there were seven other passengers in the same carriage as me, and I was the only one looking around, looking out the windows, looking at the world passing by. The other seven passengers were totally engrossed in their tiny little screens, probably being brainwashed by some would be celebrity, to go out and buy a certain range of shampoos, because it would make them feel better, or would make them more attractive than they already were.

Everybody was now a stranger just looking out for themselves. He told her that he was considering relocating to the countryside, perhaps buy a small ranch with a few horses, maybe do a bit of fishing, and just enjoy the whole "Meaning of Life" experience.

He asked her would she be interested in handling the sale of the house for him, at a nice retainer of course! 'If you like, you can freelance the transaction, which means you keep all of the commission fees, plus bear in mind that I am also looking to buy a property. You don't have to go through your company if you don't want, you make money and I save money, You do a good job for me, facilitate my needs, we both win. How does that appeal to you?'

Ross knew by the expression on Wendy's face that she was biting and it wasn't long before she took the bait. He knew he had her hooked..., hook, line and fucking sinker, just as he had thought she would be. All he needed now was the little net to pluck her out of the water. He had worked it well, even though she was an attractive and intelligent woman, he knew she was just like the fucking rest of them, interested in one thing only – *Money!*

Greed equalled money, money equalled power and power equalled greed.

In his eyes, Wendy's life was just like a carousel, like the hamster in the cage, running like the clappers, turning that wheel round and round, but it always came down to the common denominator,

"The Yankee dollar."

'If you like, we can go and have a look at the house right now,' hinted Ross.

'Maybe you can give me a rough estimation of its value and perhaps in the next couple of weeks, we can set the whole thing in motion.

I've got my car parked out back, traffic will be quiet and we can be there in fifteen minutes!'

'But you can't drive, you've been drinking, what if you get pulled over by the cops or get stopped at a checkpoint.?'

'No need to worry Wendy, it's not going to happen, you asked me earlier what I do for Uncle Sam, well if you really want to find out, come for that drive and I will enlighten you'

Although a bit hesitant at first, the couple of pink ladies in her system egged her on, and Wendy Carlisle dropped her guard, convincing herself that she was safe with this man and throwing caution to the wind, they left the bar together. It was her first mistake of the night, and for Wendy Carlisle, it would be a fatal one. Inside the car, Wendy adjusted the reclining black leather seat, stretched her legs and made herself as comfortable as possible.

'So when do I get to see what you manufacture for Uncle Sam?' asked Wendy inquisitively.

Ross turned the ignition and the 3 litre, six piston engine sprung to life.

'Okay, you watching...?' asked Ross. 'See that centre armrest by your left hand, keep your eyes on it!'

Wendy watched as Ross punched some co-ordinates into a green coloured panel on the dash board. As he did so, the sunroof and the armrest cover both slid back in unison, and to Wendy's amazement, a drone, about six maybe seven inch's in diameter appeared from inside the armrest chamber, rose up through the open sunroof and hovered about three feet above the roof of the car.

'Look at the monitor Wendy, what do you see?'

'Wow… that's fucking amazing…' yelled Wendy, 'I can see us in the car, the drone is looking down on us, as if it's watching us, okay now what?, what happens next?'

Ross punched some more co-ordinates into the dashboard panel, Wendy watched in awe as the drone rose high into the night sky before flying off in a north westerly direction ahead of the car.

'What I've done is very simple, I've programmed the co-ordinates of our planned journey to my house, the car's GPS will interact with the drone to travel the same route, however, the drone will be about three to four hundred meters ahead of us at all times, now if you look at the monitor, you will see that the drone is at present flying over 72nd St, which is about three hundred meters ahead in the distance, and as you can see, there are no images of police cars, motorcycle cops or checkpoints in that area, basically we know that we are travelling in a cop free zone and can't be apprehended even if we break the speed limit, clever yeah…!' boasted Ross.

'Yeah, but it's Friday night, the cops normally bump up their checkpoints coming into a weekend anyway, the police statistics will tell you that there are more arrests for DUI's on the weekend, what happens if there is a checkpoint on the way home, do we stop and wait for them to leave or what?'

'No no, we just take a diversion, drive down one of the side streets, go around them, then drive back onto the main street again after we have passed ahead of them. Now fasten your seatbelt, sit back and enjoy the ride!'

What a clever invention, thought Wendy, the drone was sending back live images from the air. Looking at the six inch monitor on the dashboard, they knew in advance what was around the corners and junctions some distance ahead. She had a full visual of everything that was ahead of her and Ross could take an alternative route to avoid any contact with the cops.

'Well?' asked Ross, smiling inquisitively, 'what do you think of my little surveillance gadget, at the moment we are streets ahead of any visible police activity and we have lots of options available to us in the event of any checkpoints, clever little beauty isn't she…?'

'Well to be honest Ross, if you had told me in the bar that you had this installed in your car, I would never have believed you, not in a million years!

Are these available to buy, I mean are they part of the car specification or do you buy and install it yourself?' asked Wendy, still not quite sure what she made of it all.

'You can't do neither,' answered Ross, 'this is a prototype model that I have been experimenting with for some time, I've installed this one myself and the company hasn't made a decision just yet on when we will be putting it on the market, maybe at a later stage perhaps, but for now it's just a personal toy that I use to get me around without detection, stay under the radar if you know what I mean…'

'Gee Ross, you must think you're a spy…,' giggled Wendy.

'You can laugh all you want Wendy, but this is a serious piece of equipment that I will be testing over the coming months, it's all part of a project that I am starting, all part of a daring plan that I am putting into place!'

'And are you confident that your daring plan is going to work?' asked Wendy.

'Oh don't worry Wendy,' answered Ross, continuing to cajole his prey, 'this project is going to be a huge success, in fact I am so confident of its success that I would like to include you in the greater scheme of things, would you like that?'

'You want to include me in the plan..? how are you going to manage that? do I need to sign a non-disclosure document or something' joked Wendy, 'or do I get paid for keeping it a secret, is it even legal what you're doing? However, I am intrigued, I need you to tell me everything' Wendy said, convincing herself that they were now partners in some exciting and dangerous adventure, totally oblivious to the precarious situation she was putting herself in.

'Oh don't worry' said Ross, 'all will be revealed soon, you know what Wendy? let's get back to my place where we can relax, then I will explain what I have in mind.'

Ross steered the 3L machine through the opening black metal gates, cruised up the drive, the car coming to a halt about one foot from the bottom steps that led up to the house. He then pressed some buttons on the dash and once again the armrest and sunroof opened in unison.

Looking up, Wendy could now see the drone was hovering about five feet directly above the car, it was like a pet dog that had been let off its lead for a run, and was now waiting for its master to catch up, pat it on the head, before putting it back in its box.

The drone positioned itself above the sunroof, hovered for a couple of seconds before descending slowly into the armrest chamber, the armrest and sunroof again closing in unison.

Although the journey home went as planned, Ross was pleased, there was no traffic congestion, the streets and the sidewalks were relatively quiet, but more importantly, the drone had done its job and was now safely back in its box.

'Wow…' purred Wendy, as she slid out of the car and looked up at the house,

'This is some mansion, with the gardens and everything it must be worth somewhere in the region of four million dollars, however…' lingered Wendy, 'experience has taught me not to judge a house by the colour of its front door, I can't wait to step inside and check out the interior decor,' quipped Wendy as they threaded carefully up the ice covered steps.

The cold January night air had a sharpness about it, its chilled crisp wind bit into the cheeks of Wendy Carlisle's face. She looked upwards in awe, the clear sky revealing the constellation of stars that made up "The Big Dipper". She gave a shiver as she linked her right arm in around Ross's muscular biceps, feeling the warmth of his body as they approached the front door.

22

Still aware of the humming noise coming from the freezer in the background, Wendy remembers entering through the main doors and standing in the spacious hallway, staring in admiration of the magnificent baroque style sculptural pieces that stood in line along the hallway, like a guard of honour, and beautifully lit up by the huge glass crystal chandelier hanging from the ceiling. The walls were draped with oak framed oil paintings and a Victorian studio couch rested neatly in the corner.

Ross ushered Wendy into the large sitting room lounge, where even more paintings that were oil painted on canvas stared back at her.

'Gin and ice?' asked Ross, shaking a whiskey glass temptingly in her face.

'Oh, go on then' replied Wendy, still in awe of the room she was standing in. What beautiful treasures she thought to herself, the old oak designed furniture filling the four corners of the room, the art pieces practically dripping down the walls, little curios placed conveniently along the allocated floor space nearest to the walls. Wendy looked up and marvelled at the fresco of Mount Rushmore and its four Presidents who were looking down on her from the ceiling.

It was as if she was standing in the middle of a crowd, mixing in the company of Pablo Picasso, Claude Monet and Vincent Van Gogh.

Wendy had sold hundreds of different properties over the past couple of years, but none of them compared or even came close to the magnificent mansion she now found herself standing in. The conservatory which was located on the east wing of the house, was probably worth a half a million bucks on its own. She now understood what Ross had meant when he described it as his

Shangri-La. Yes it was certainly a stand alone mansion, managing the sale of this beauty would enhance her profile no end, this would be her jewel in the crown, plus the commission on the sale would be huge, in fact as she looked across the room at Ross, she thought to herself that if she played her cards right tonight, she might possibly reel in the big prize for herself.

While Wendy was dreaming about the possibilities that were opening up for her, Ross was placing a large drink in her hand,

'I hope Bourbon is okay?' he asked, placing his hand on her left shoulder and squeezing it gently, 'out of gin at the moment.'

Their glass's clinked and Ross took a hefty swig as they both sat on a studio couch.

Wendy lifted the glass to her lips, took a sip of the bourbon and swirled it about in her mouth, like a wine connoisseur would caress and analyse a nineteen fifties claret.

'I gotta say Ross, I am hugely impressed, if the rest of the house is anything to go by, and from what I've seen already…, we could be looking at a selling price somewhere between five and a half to six million dollars.'

'Now I'm the one that's impressed!' Ross said.

'That's not bad Wendy, not bad at all.'

'What's not bad?'

'Your valuation, it's pretty bang on, I had it valued only last week and they came in with around the same selling price!'

'Well, what can I say? Wendy said, raising her hands in the air, as if acknowledging the wisdom of her valuation, and feeling quite pleased with herself.

'Fancy a top up?' she asked.

'Yeah, why not' Ross answered.

'The bar never closes in this house!'

Wendy filled the two glasses with generous measures,

'Got any more ice?' she asked.

'Yeah, there's another ice bucket in the miniature fridge under the bar top, but I won't have any ice this time, I'll just have it neat.'

As the night progressed, they talked about everything, college, property, ambitions, while classical music played in the background.

With the minutes ticking by, Wendy wondered whether Ross was going to make a move on her at all, she was alone with this hunk, in his house, playing by his rules and as of yet, no signs, no signals of intimate foreplay, nothing. At one point it had crossed her mind that he might be gay, but dismissed that possibility out of hand almost immediately.

She had decided that if he did make a move on her, she would not resist, and if he didn't..., then she would have to take the lead, make the first move. She had already conjured up a scenario in her head where she would make a move on him, slowly seduce him, put on a performance that he could not resist. Why not? she asked herself..., she could do slutty just as bad as the next girl, she could act undignified, she could be trashy! As she fantasized on her next move, she glanced across at the framed painting of Rebecca, thinking to herself that whatever Rebecca could do, she could do better! There was without doubt, a situation here that could be exploited to her advantage and she wasn't prepared to let it slip through her fingers! Whatever it would take, she was game, she would rise to it. This could be the biggest deal of her career, a once in a lifetime opportunity and she wasn't going to fuck it up!

After she had finished her third drink, Wendy began to feel a little lightheaded and was having trouble lifting and moving her arms and legs. She tried to stand up, but her limbs refused to obey her brain, as if she was paralysed. It was then she realised that she only had body movement from the neck up, the rest of her body was numb and in a state of paralysis.

'Ross, I don't feel too good right now, I don't know if it's the amount of alcohol I've had or maybe it's because I've eaten very little today, but I don't seem to be able to move my arms or legs, I feel like I'm having some kind of stroke!'

Ross leaned across towards Wendy, his nostrils inhaling the bewitching fragrance of her perfume, his lips almost caressing her earlobes as he whispered softly in her ear, 'Don't worry Wendy, you're not having a stroke, it's just the nerve toxin kicking in...'

'What nerve toxin?' Wendy asked, the alarm bells now starting to ring, starting to get a little louder.

'What have you done to me, you bastard, have you drugged me?'

Ross put his index finger close to his mouth, indicating to Wendy that he wanted her to be quiet.

'It's a common compound called Curare, it comes from a plant extract sourced in South America, the natives apply it to the tip of their arrows or blowgun darts to paralyse their prey. It simply blocks out the information that your nerves send to your muscles and given the correct dosage, it can shut down your complete, well almost complete muscular system.'

'Is it going to kill me?' asked Wendy.

'No, it won't, but you will be incapacitated for a couple of hours.'

'But how did you manage to drug me? I was watching you all of the time, was it in the bar? was it here? How?'

'Simple, it was the Bourbon.'

'The bourbon..., but how?' she asked.

'We both drank from the same bottle, I poured the drinks myself...'

'You cunning bastard! It was the ice wasn't it? It was the fucking ice!'

'You drank your's neat!'

'Yes Wendy, it was the ice' Ross said, a wry smile appearing across his face.

'I mixed the toxin with water earlier today and put it in the ice box freezer. Actually speaking of freezers, I want to introduce you to someone later, shall we say, an old acquaintance of mine...'

Wendy could sense that the tone of Ross's voice had changed to a more sinister one, his eyes had turned cold and dark and the atmosphere had turned frosty. She couldn't comprehend how just minutes earlier she had been in the company of a handsome silver tongued devil who oozed charisma at every turn and had suddenly turned into a monster. Wendy was now terrified and fearful for her life.

'Why have you done this to me? are you going to rape me? are you going to *kill* me...?'

'To be honest Wendy, I don't think you really want to know your fate at the moment, I know exactly what's going to happen to you..., by the way, do you remember during the drive home, we spoke about this little project I had in mind, you were so eager to be involved, you were so keen you actually suggested signing non disclosure agreements and I remembered saying to myself, 'Fuck!! This woman is perfect, what a way to start my little game, my little game of cat and mouse, you see Wendy, I've got a confession to make, I've got a weakness, sometimes I like to do things on impulse, over the years, I've done some nasty impulsive things and they have worked okay for me, in fact the adrenalin rush that surges through my body is phenomenal, adrenalin has surely got to be the most complete class A drug on the market today and it's our own bodies that stimulates it, fascinating isn't it?'

'Who are you? what do you want from me?' sobbed Wendy, the fear rushing through her body at the thought that she might not survive the night.

'We've never met before tonight, I've never done you any harm, up to tonight you had no idea who I was, who I worked for, or where I lived!'

'Ah...' interrupted Ross, his index finger pointing at her as he waved his hand in the air.

'That's where you're wrong Wendy..., I know everything about you, tonight was not just a chance meeting..., I've been planning this for weeks, I know your name, address, your small circle of friends, I have been following you on social media, in fact I know your age and your date of birth, you're a Capricorn, aren't you?'

'Yes I am, but how do you know? why do you ask?'

'How do I know?' asked Ross. 'I'll tell you how I know, your best friend has told me everything about you, in fact she couldn't stop talking about you.'

'What best friend...?'

'Why Susan of course, she couldn't stop talking about you, do you know that those born under the Zodiac sign of Capricorn are determined and ambitious people, they want to be successful in life, no free handouts, no, not for Capricorns, their ambitions are boundless, without limits, and their achievements will always match their ambitions at the very least. The manner in which Susan spoke about you, I had you figured as a Capricorn ever before she told me your date of birth.'

'How do you know Susan?'

'How do I know Susan? You've gotta be kidding! Susan and I have known each other a couple of years now, you see Wendy, I'm Susan's Boss!'

'*What!* I don't believe you!'

'Susan and I have a very good working relationship, and a couple of weeks back, just before Christmas she was going around the office, showing photographs and videos of a thirtieth birthday party of one of her friends, that friend was you Wendy, and I immediately took a liking to you. I could have picked any of Susan's friends in the video to initiate my plans but..., I chose you Wendy, I chose you, you were absolutely perfect for me!!'

'I've watched both of you at the bar for the last two Friday evenings, chatting, giggling, looking, checking out the young guys as they passed by. I knew you would be at the bar tonight, I knew you would be waiting for Susan, but I also knew she would not be turning up, you see Wendy, it was I who sent Susan the email telling her she would have to work late, there was no emergency..., there was no client in trouble, it was sent solely to ensure that you would be on your own in the bar tonight!'

'But..., how come Susan never mentioned your name to me before, she talked about a few of her office colleagues in passing, but she never mentioned you in any conversation, never...!'

'Well that's good to know, answered Ross, 'you see Wendy, because of the secretive nature of our business and the security threats we get from time to time, the company has a very basic rule for all its employees. Outside the four walls of the company you don't talk about your job and you don't reveal the names of your work colleagues to anybody!

This rule is incorporated into every employee's contract, break that rule, you break your contract, in other words you will be fired, your name put on a renegade list sent to every large corporation across the globe. End result, you will never work at that level again, in fact, you would be lucky to get a job on a street vendor's cart.

Well, hasn't tonight worked out very nicely, what do you think Wendy...?'

Wendy was now starting to sweat, beads of perspiration starting to form across her forehead, but try as hard as she might, she was powerless to wipe them clear.

'Okay, enough of the chit chat' said Ross, 'I have to be up early in the morning, going for a round of golf with some influential friends, so we need to get our sleep. I guess in the situation you're in, I will have to carry you to your bedroom which by the way is downstairs in the basement.

Anyway don't worry, you won't be alone down there, you won't be short of company that's for sure.'

Ross bent over Wendy and picked her up, casually throwing her over his right shoulder as if she were a rag doll.

Down in the basement, he sat her on a chair and bound both hands together with nylon tie-wraps, then using another tie- wrap, he securely bound both hands to the three inch steel pipe that ran down the side of the wall.

'Now my dear Wendy,' whispered Ross into her ear, 'try and get some sleep, we've got a busy day tomorrow...'

23

As the precious minutes tick by, Wendy realises that if she doesn't free herself soon, she is going to die, she tries to yank her hands free from the tie wraps that imprison her but to no avail, she even attempts to bite through the nylon wraps but her teeth make no impact whatsoever. She can still hear the scurrying of her furry little friends, running in all directions across the basement floor. She prays that her mind is playing tricks with her but it seems the noise and the scurrying is getting louder and closer, maybe they're circling the wagons, maybe they have put together a plan to attack from all angles so as to render her weak and defenceless, in a position where she will put up little or no resistance.

Maybe it's just the food on the plate that they are after, perhaps they will be content with just the meat. What if they devour everything and still want more?

Her wrists are now starting to bleed so it's also possible they can already smell the blood, any minute now there could be an all out frenzied attack.

Using her head, she could nudge the plate onto the floor and hopefully they would just eat and retreat, but she doesn't think so. She knows they won't be content with what they've eaten from the plate. To them, that will have been the starter, now they will want to sample the main course. Wendy looks at her wrists again, her efforts to bite the nylon wraps has made no difference, her teeth have become loose and her gums are starting to bleed, yet still the tie-wraps remain tightly secure.

There was only one way that those tie-wraps were going to break, it was a crazy idea, but right now it was the only one she had, if it works she has a chance of staying alive, if it doesn't, she's dead anyway...

Wendy starts to pick up the bacon and sausage pieces with her teeth, rubbing and spreading the meat along her wrists, slowly chewing into the tie wraps themselves, mixing the meat with the nylon. she also spits some pieces from her mouth onto the piping that runs along the wall.

Wendy knows she's taking a big risk depending on how many rats have made the basement their home, but her insane idea is the only option that's available to her.

She could wait for Ross to return and take her chance on somehow overpowering him, but she is tired, she is weak, she knows she will lose the fight, however if the rats are hungry enough, not only will they eat the meat they will also gnaw their way through the nylon, as they gobble up every morsel of food that's available.

She's hoping that they will chew through the nylon, weakening its hold just enough that she will be able to break the bind.

For fifteen minutes, Wendy Carlisle didn't move a muscle, not even when she felt the sensation of soft rodent fur brushing against her ankles and feet as she stood in almost total darkness.

She senses that the squealing sounds are not as loud as before, the patter of feet have almost come to a standstill, they're ready!, she thinks, the fucker's are ready and are now in a position to attack, maybe they're waiting on the orders of the great King Rat himself, to advance on their prey and begin the feeding frenzy.

Wendy anticipated that something was going to happen soon, she placed the palms of her hands around the upright water pipe, clenched her hands tightly together, closing her eyes as she did so.

As the minutes went by, Wendy would experience her worst living nightmare, she could now hear the patter of their little feet travelling hurriedly along the water pipes, quickly devouring the pieces of food that blocked their path, knowing that they would eventually make their way to the feast.

It wasn't long before she could feel the nudging of sharp teeth on her skin, nervously flinching her fingers while the rodents moved in on the prize, the scent of warm flesh welcoming them to the banquet.

This was it, she thought, if she was going to break free it was going to be in the next couple of minutes, the feeding frenzy had begun and there must have been seven, maybe eight rats fighting for the remaining scraps.

The rats were now climbing all over her hands and wrists gnawing away at whatever smelled and tasted like food. Wendy was now experiencing real pain as the rats nibbled into her flesh, but she could also sense that the wraps around her wrists were beginning to loosen a little, she had heard about rodents gnawing their way through electric cables, wiring, causing power outages and she was hoping this was the reason for the slackness she felt on her wrists.

With the frenzied onslaught continuing at a frantic pace and in so much pain, Wendy wasn't sure what was going to give way first, the nylon wraps or her will to live. When she finally managed to pluck up the courage to open her eyes, she stared in utter disbelief, letting out a loud pitched scream at the horror that was unveiling before her eyes. About a dozen rats were now crawling around her hands and wrists, biting and gnawing at her open flesh, devouring anything with blood on it.

Now in a rage of pure insanity, Wendy let out one last scream, and with one almighty effort with what strength she had left, she gave one final yank at breaking the wraps and to her astonishment, the nylon wraps snapped open and she fell to her knees.

The rats sensing the banquet was over, for now at least, quickly dispersed, retreating back into the darkened corners from where they had come.

Wendy looked at her wrists, they were still bleeding profusely and she needed to stop the flow of blood immediately. She quickly headed for the stairs, but when she got to the top of the stairway, she discovered that the door was locked from the outside. She instinctively banged on the door and screamed, yelling out at the top of her voice, but to no avail, nobody it appeared was coming to her rescue.

Wendy assumed that the house was still empty and that Ross had not yet returned. She descended back down the stairs, where her first priority now was to stop the bleeding. She took a bottle of wine from the wine rack, uncorking it before helping herself to a huge swig to quench her thirst. She then poured the rest of the wine over her wrists, in the hope that the alcohol would in some way sterilise the wounds.

Looking around the basement, Wendy found some small flannel towels which she used as bandages, tying them tightly above her wrists to stem the flow of blood. It was obvious to Wendy that she needed urgent medical treatment for her wounds, and needed it fast. She didn't want to panic, she knew if she remained calm, her chances of survival would increase.

Having freed herself once, Wendy convinced herself that she had the strength and the resolve to do it again.

She would have to wait until Ross returned, confront him there and then, or perhaps create some kind of diversion, something that would give her the opportunity to surprise and overcome her would be killer.

Wendy now wished that herself and Susan had continued with those self defence classes that they had signed up for a couple of months ago, it had been for a six month programme but they had only endured it for about six weeks as life itself had got in the way. She was still a fit woman and reckoned that even those six weeks basic training might just be enough to help her escape. She could pretend that she was still securely bound to the pipes and when Ross came down to the basement she would have the element of surprise.

There were some heavy wooden planks stored in the corner of the basement, maybe she could use one of those as a weapon, she had no idea of what time it was, but guessed it was late afternoon and it was possible that Ross would be returning sometime soon.

The flannel towels that she had wrapped around her wrists seemed to be working as the blood flow slowed to a minimum. Wendy continued to explore what the basement had to offer in terms of self defence options. Although the L shaped basement was dimly lit, Wendy was able to walk around with relative ease.

She sifted through some old furniture pieces stacked against the wall, there were several oil paintings scattered across the floor on the other side of the wall, most of them portraits of a beautiful young woman, and close by, there was another smaller wine rack with half a dozen bottles stored on it. Across in the other corner was an old rocking chair that had clearly seen better days and she noticed that one of the back supports was hanging off, barely held together by a rusty screw.

Wendy pulled at the back support and it came away freely, it was a heavy piece, probably made of oak or mahogany and could be the ideal weapon in her quest for freedom.

Now that she had something worth defending herself with, Wendy felt a resurgence of energy shooting through her body instilling confidence that she would somehow get out of the basement alive.

She walked towards the humming noise and stopped at the freezer, she lifted the lid ever so gently and almost toppled backwards, screaming louder than anything she had done earlier.

Recovering her balance, she stepped forward again and slowly peeped in over the top of the freezer, her eyes met Rebecca's and they both stared at each other for a couple of seconds, as if in a stand off, with Wendy being the first to blink.

Rebecca's cold blue eyes just stared back at her from gaps between the ice bags.

Trying to remain as calm as she could, Wendy pushed aside the packs of frozen vegetables and the bags of ice to reveal the full naked identity of Rebecca Kingsley.

Although her face was a patchy blue colour, there was no doubt that the face Wendy was looking down at was the same as the one with the youthful rosy cheeks smiling from the oil paintings that lay on the ground close by. Wendy was no fashion expert but she would guess that the clothes worn by the woman in the portraits were at least fifteen years old if not more. It all started to make sense now, his wife Rebecca did not die on 9/11. He killed her and faked her death – and he had gotten away with it!

The thought that Ross had kept a dead woman's body in a freezer for such a long period of time sent an ice cold shiver down her spine. Why did he kill her, did she discover that she was married to a psychopath, Whatever the reason, she had ended up dead. Wendy wasn't quite sure, it just didn't make sense, how would you be able to hide a body, especially your wife's in a freezer, in a basement all this time without the police finding it.

When he reported her missing, surely the first thing the cops would have done was to search the house, and certainly the basement to rule out the owner as a suspect.

Wendy looked down at her wrists and saw that they were bleeding again, although not profusely, this was good she thought, the main arteries had not been severed as much as she had thought, she could still do this, she just needed to believe that she would walk away from this madness, escape from the clutches of this psychopath.

Just at that moment, her body froze, and she gave out a sharp cry, she moved closer to one of the ventilation shafts on the wall and listened intently. She could hear the sound of a car engine thundering up the drive, the tyres eventually screeching to a halt, close to the steps in front of the house.

'Fuck!!, he's back!!, what the fuck am I suppose to do now?' Wendy asked herself, trying to control her breathing. She had started to hyperventilate, the fear of his return almost suffocating her, she inhaled and exhaled in short breaths which helped to relax her breathing, as she frantically searched for a safe place to hide.

Wendy got into position and crouched down low, her heart palpitations rapidly increasing as she listened to the rattling of keys on the other side of the basement door. She had been crouched in that position for about ten minutes, waiting for him, and she was ready. She looked towards the stairway, as the door creaked open, the reflection of light brightening up the basement.

It wasn't hard to make out the dark silhouette figure that was standing at the top of the stairs, it was Ross, he was just standing there without moving, not making a sound. There was complete silence, the freezer had stopped humming, even the rats that had devoured her soft flesh earlier, had now deserted her. They obviously had seen this before.

Ross switched on the basement lights and slowly descended down the wooden stairs one step at a time. Wendy was keeping her eyes firmly on him when suddenly, he stopped, turned around and began to walk back up the stairs again.

'What the fuck is he doing now? why doesn't he come down and look for me?' Wendy asked herself.

When Ross reached the top of the stairs, he put the key back in the keyhole and locked it shut from the inside. It was obvious to him that Wendy had broken free, and was now hiding somewhere in the basement. Now it was time for the cat and mouse game to begin, it was time for the cat to hunt down his prey. Ross began his descent down into the cellar for the second time. He was disappointed and furious with himself that she had managed to break free from what he had thought was a secure binding of her hands and wrists.

He knew however that in the L shaped basement, there was only one door, meaning there was only one way in and only one way out.

As the door was locked shut when he arrived, he knew that Wendy was still in the basement, hiding in some corner waiting to pounce. Ross decided to tease her for a little while, have some fun with his quarry.

'Hey Wendy, do you want to play some games, how about hide and seek? Yes, hide and seek would be good, wouldn't it Wendy…?' Ross asked teasingly.

'I'll tell you what, let's make it interesting, the door at the top of the stairs is the door to your future but right now it is locked, these are the keys' he shouted as he rattled the bunch of them on his right index finger. Ross turned towards the stairs, and threw them through the air, the keys hitting against the door, before landing on the top step. 'Only one of us will open that door,' shouted Ross as he pulled a pair of gloves from his pocket, slowly covering his fingers and hands with the soft white cotton material, as if anticipating what was going to happen next.

'If you manage to reach the top of the stairs and open the door, it will mean you are free, but if I open it, it will mean that you die, that's the reality of the situation, those are the facts Wendy, are you up for it…!!?'

Ross waited for an answer but there was no reply, only silence,

'Okay sweetheart, it's time to play, let the fun begin!'

Wendy kept her breathing to a minimum, she was doing her utmost to remain calm as she cowered low, waiting…, waiting for the opportunity which would give her an advantage over her predator.

Ross slowly walked across the basement floor, his eyes focusing on the areas where he thought she might be hiding. As he moved closer to the L shaped corner, he could just make out what seemed like an arm and hand drooping over the side of the chair's armrest, Wendy's opal bracelet on her wrist reflecting brightly in the light. Ross wondered was she already dead, maybe she was just unconscious, having fainted from the shock of her ordeal.

He hoped she wasn't dead, he didn't want Wendy to have the last say in her death, it was not the way he had planned it, she was to die by his hands, and his hands only!

This made him angry and that impulsive rage that was simmering inside him was now coming to the boil again, he picked a bottle of wine from the wine rack, brushed the dust off the label which revealed a 1969 red grape Californian delight, such a shame to waste it like this, not too many of those left on wine racks across the world, he thought to himself as he smashed the wine bottle against the wall, the Merlot flowing down the wall like a river of warm blood.

Ross moved stealthily, tiptoeing across the basement floor, keeping his eyes fixed on Wendy's drooping arm, which hadn't moved a muscle when he had smashed the bottle against the wall.

Because the basement was L shaped, as he moved slowly closer to Wendy, he still couldn't see her face, just her arm and hand protruding from her jacket. He was now standing on the opposite side of the wall, if he was able to put his hand through the brick work that separated them, he would be catching her around the throat. He estimated, that with Wendy sitting down, her upper torso would be at the same height as his waist, and her head would be a couple of inches above that.

It was time, he thought to himself, it was time to end it now, he would not prolong her suffering any longer, and as he moved closer to the edge, he swiftly lunged his body and his left hand around to the other side of the wall, but to his horror, the jagged edged bottle just bounced off the body and fell to the floor.

For a couple of seconds, Ross stared in shock and disbelief, the person sitting in the chair looking up at him was not Wendy, but his dead wife Rebecca…

When Ross had arrived back at the house earlier, Wendy knew that he would be heading straight for the basement, so she had pulled Rebecca's stiff body from the freezer, put her jacket on the corpse, slipped the bracelet on her wrist and placed her on the chair, close to the wall.

'WENDY… YOU FUCKING BITCH!!' shouted Ross, who was in a state of shock, his disbelieving eyes staring at Rebecca sitting in the chair. With whatever resolve she had left, Wendy dashed from her hiding place and using the armrest as her weapon, delivered a heavy blow to Ross's skull, and he fell to his knees, dazed. Wendy seized her chance and ran towards the stairway. With her strength now diminishing rapidly, she raced to the top of the stairs, picked the set of keys off the ground, fumbling with them as she put them in the lock. The first two attempts were unsuccessful, and as she put the third key in the lock, she looked around to see that Ross was slowly getting to his feet. Still fumbling, Wendy managed to turn the key and the lock bolt clicked to the left and she pushed the door open. It was her intention to lock Ross in the basement but she never got the chance. As she turned to push the door closed, Ross came at her with a lunge and they both fell to the floor. He was now sitting on top of her, his strong hands firmly squeezing the whole of her neck, while pressing down on her throat.

As much as she tried, Wendy was unable to put up a resistance, although she was gasping for breath, she had used up all the energy she had left, she had no more to give. In a way she was glad, soon her nightmare would be over. As Ross's strong hands tightened on their powerful grip around her throat, she looked up at the deranged contorted expression on his face, stared into his cold evil eyes and smiled.

If she was going to die, it would be on her terms, not his, Wendy then closed her eyes, relinquishing all hopes of staying alive as a dark grey mist descended upon her, and the beat of her heart was no more.

24

January 2019

Lieutenant Max Hammond stood close to the edge of the overgrown embankment, the fingers and thumb of his right hand rubbing hard against the tough bristles on his chin. He was looking down at the young female body that lay at his feet, exposed to the cold slushy snow on the ground.

Although there had been a flurry of snow earlier, it did not conceal the apparent brutality endured by the victim. The young woman's hands and feet were bound, and although her face was badly beaten, it was clear by the marks around her neck, that probable cause of death would be asphyxiation by strangulation. Even though her eyes were closed, Max could sense the fear and horror that she had endured during her grim demise.

'Anybody got ID yet?' Max asked, to no one in particular.

'The victim's name is Wendy Carlisle.' Pete answered,

'She was reported missing the day before yesterday, a real estate executive, worked for a property management company called East Side Properties, funnily enough it was her ID card that was pinned to her lapel which told us who she was.'

'And why would that be funny?' Max asked.

'Well' said Pete, 'I've spoken to her friend Susan Carter, the girl who reported her missing, they were to meet up last Friday night in a bar called "The Bootleggers" but, because of unexpected work commitments, Susan never turned up. She said the victim never wore her ID on her lapel, she always carried it in her bag and she never brought her work to the bar.'

'So why is it pinned to her lapel now?' asked Max.

'That's what we have to figure out, maybe she had a late viewing appointment with a client, maybe she was closing a deal after office hours.'

'What about transport? did she have a car?'

'Yeah, it's parked up in the car lot at the back of the bar, Susan has confirmed that it's the victim's car.

'Get someone to check in with her office manager, see what her itinerary was for Friday, in fact get a list of all the viewing appointments she had honoured for the week, I want a list of all the clients she met, and also a list of any cancellations she may have had.'

Max used his pen to flick the ID card over on its back,

'Have you seen this Pete?'

'Seen what?'

'It looks like a verse that someone has printed and attached to her ID card. It might be something and it might be nothing, but check it out, it could be just words of sentimental value to our victim,'

'And if not?' Pete asked.

'Then it would appear our killer may have left his first calling card with many more to come!'

'Where the hell are Forensics?'

'They're on the way boss, they should be here soon,' answered Pete.

'When we're finished here I want to interview the victim's friend Susan Carter, get her into the office, let's see if she can shed any light on this, also we need to contact the victim's next of kin and break the bad news to them.'

As Max stooped down to take a closer look at the body, he noticed that some of the flesh on Wendy's wrists had split open and the blood had hardened, it was unusual and nothing like what Max had seen in over twenty years on the job.

'That's strange,' he whispered to himself, 'the nylon tie wraps are secure, no doubt about that, but there is no way that the wraps could have caused those injuries.' It looked like the flesh had been torn open, maybe by a jagged weapon of some sort, he would leave that to the experts in forensics who by their absence up to now, was beginning to irritate him.

A cold breeze caressed Max's face as he looked upwards, scanning the immediate area, checking to see if there were any CCTV cameras in the vicinity, even though he knew in all probability there were none.

It was just an old habit acquired over the years, experience had taught him that you gotta tick all the boxes at a crime scene, leave nothing to chance.

The location where the body was found, was in the middle of a shaded and secluded area, surrounded by trees, patches of shrubbery and close to the river. The killer could have transported the body either by boat or canoe under the cover of darkness and would still have avoided been spotted.

Max had visited a lot of crime scenes over the years, he had come face to face with many dead bodies, people who had died of gunshot wounds, knife wounds or strangulation, the routine stuff, but this was without doubt one of the worse murder scenarios that he had ever encountered.

There was something evil about the manner in which this young woman had been murdered, this wasn't a random killing, from what he could see there were no visible signs of sexual assault, her purse was unopened, bank and credit cards seemed to be intact and there was roughly one hundred dollars still in her wallet. It was possible that the victim knew her killer. It was also evidently clear, given the fact that there was no attempt to conceal the body, the killer wanted the body to be found. The question was why?

Max was sitting on the bark of an old cedar tree, looking over the embankment on the edge of the river, every now and again, a thin layer of ice would float past, reminding him that it was still early January. He was deep in thought, familiarising himself with the enclosed area, absorbing everything and anything relating to the crime scene, when the forensics team appeared from around a clump of pine trees.

'Hello Max, I thought you didn't work on the sabbath any more...?' shouted Sharon, looking as radiant as ever as she used both hands to push her dark silk hair back behind her ears.

'How are you today?' she asked, 'we've got to stop meeting like this or people will start to talk about us again!,'

'Yes they might,' answered Max, briefly reminiscing on times long past, when he and Sharon had lived together. It had been a torrid relationship, a merging of high intensity, they were both strong driven individuals, only problem was, sometimes they were driven in opposite directions. For Max, every case he had worked on became something of a crusade, not letting anything or anyone get in the way of his investigations, not until at least a positive arrest had been made. Sharon, on the other hand would delve deeply into her work, ensuring everything was done by the book, dotting the I's, crossing the T's, however, the one thing they did have in common above all else, was their obsession in bringing closure for victims and their families, ensuring that those responsible, were brought to justice, paying dearly for their crimes.

The relationship lasted less than two years with Sharon eventually moving back to her parent's house. Max's reminiscence of the past was quickly interrupted by Sharon's voice.

'First impressions would suggest that our victim died from strangulation, choked to death by someone during an uncontrolled rage, however the multiple cuts and bruising on her hands and wrists, the loss of blood would suggest that something horrible occurred before she died.

Max nodded in agreement.

'Approximate time of death?'

'Judging by the blood settlement around both her wrists, and the colour of the bruising around her neck, I would hazard a guess and say that she died sometime in the last twelve to twenty four hours, Rigor Mortis is clearly evident but no signs of dissipation just yet, off the record I would hazard a guess and put a time of around 5 pm yesterday evening. I'll be able to give you a more accurate time frame once I carry out the post mortem.

'What about the wrists Sharon? asked Max,

'what can you tell me about the wrists?'

'Well those types of injuries are rare but are not new to me, it looks like they were chewed or gnawed on, definitely before the body was placed here, again I will know more after the autopsy, however I can tell you that this was the second time that her wrists were bound. Sharon pointed to the bruising around the area of the metacarpus and the wrists,

'See those marks, there's no doubt that she was bound and tied at least twice, possibly with the same type of nylon tie-wrap.'

'Seems odd,' Max said.

'Why would her killer have to bind her twice?' why would he have to do that?'

'Looking at the messy bits around the wrists, bits of flesh missing, I think I know the answer to your question, but I will let you know for sure tomorrow morning.'

'Great!, I'll send Pete over around 11am tomorrow to collect the autopsy report, or maybe I could drop over for them myself…, maybe we could catch up on things,' hinted Max, giving the impression that he was eager for them to possibly renew their relationship, carry on where they left off.

'Tell Pete the autopsy report will be ready for collection around noon' answered Sharon as she went meticulously about her gory business, her microscopic eyes not shifting from the job in hand.

'Can we possibly get it earlier? Max asked,

'We know how she died, it's not exactly rocket science, is it?'

'No Max, you're right, it's not rocket science, it's forensic science, which is why you won't get my report until at least midday tomorrow.'

'Well, that told me' thought Max to himself, 'maybe she's already moved on to greener pastures, maybe she's found someone else, someone that she could rely on. I certainly won't be going down that fucking road again!' he was thinking to himself as he waded his way through the melting snow, back towards his car.

'Hey Pete, don't forget to contact the victim's friend Susan Carter, have her in my office at around three this afternoon, I want to talk her through her statement, maybe prompt her into remembering something she may have forgotten, or unwittingly left out, something she thought wasn't relevant, and if all that fails, perhaps with our last throw of the dice she might be able to shed some light on the verse printed on the victims ID, oh... and by the way, before I forget... can you collect the victim's autopsy report from the coroners office around midday tomorrow.'

Although their personnel lives had left a few scars on both of them, Max nonetheless, freely acknowledged that Sharon was a pathologist of great distinction. He had no doubt that the autopsy and forensic report compiled by her and her team at the lab would be clear and concise. One could always be confident, that any report with Sharon Stillman's signature at the bottom, would be flawless, totally airtight from any scrutiny from a defending lawyer, in fact, rumour had it that when any of the state attorney's had a wet dream thinking about convincing a jury to bring back a guilty verdict for a murder rap, Sharon Stillman would have played some part in it.

25

Max and Pete entered the interview room just after 3 p.m. Pete closing the door behind them. Susan Carter was just sitting there, her head bowed, her eyes looking towards the floor. The young woman looked pretty shook up, the crumpled wet tissues on the tabled indicated that she had been crying for some time. It was Pete who spoke first.

'Hello Susan, thank you for coming in to talk to us, this is Lieutenant Max Hammond, he's the lead investigator into the death of your friend Wendy.

'Hi Susan,' said Max,

'We really do appreciate you coming in to talk to us in what is a very hard time for you I'm sure, we'll try not to keep you too long.'

'What's your full Name?'

'Susan Ellen Carter'

'Address?'

'66, Fairbanks Avenue.'

'Date of Birth?'

'October 12th, Nineteen eighty nine.'

'Age?'

'Thirty years old.'
'Occupation?'

'Senior Electronic Engineer,

ame**RK**omm Telecommunications.'

'How long were you and Wendy friends and when did you both first meet?'

'We first met briefly about eight years ago in College where we both attended a specific lecture, but it wasn't until we bumped into each other at the "Fitness for Hire" gym on West Street about two years ago that we started hanging out together, we talked about our jobs, our hobbies, stuff like that, and we just seemed to hit it off.'

'Boyfriends?'

'Yeah, we both dated guys from time to time, nothing serious, at least nothing long term.'

'What about stalkers? Anybody using threatening behaviour to either of you on social media outlets?'

'No nothing!, we were just two ordinary girls having a good time, just enjoying life, we met religiously every Friday night, same bar, same time.

'What was the name of the bar.?' Max asked.

"The Bootleggers" answered Susan, 'it's in Queens, on twenty first street, best bar in town, especially on a Friday night!'

'But last Friday night, you girls did not meet up, correct?'

'Yes, I couldn't make it, something urgent came up at work and my boss said I had to stay back and put it right.'

'But you did manage to speak to Wendy?'

'Yes I did, and to be honest, I thought she would be mad at me for missing our date, but she wasn't, and I actually got the impression that she was happy that I wasn't going to make it.'

'What gave you that impression?' asked Pete.

'I don't know, it was something in her voice, it was as if she was talking to me but her concentration was elsewhere, as if she was with somebody and couldn't wait for me to hang up, that was it.

I called her on her mobile yesterday evening and this morning, but no answer.'

'Was the phone ringing out when you made the calls,' asked Max.

'No, there was nothing, it was if she had turned off her phone, or maybe the battery was dead.'

'Did you or Wendy ever do drugs, something to give you a lift for the weekend, a bit of coke maybe…?' Max asked.

'No Sir, we were both clean, I know it seems to be the fashionable thing to do these days but, we never touched that shit, we were just two bubbly outgoing girls, looking to enjoy life.'

Susan reached for another tissue as the tears ran down her face. Max pushed Wendy's ID card across the table in front of her hoping that because they were such close friends, she might be able to decipher or decode the meaning of the words.

'Does this mean anything to you Susan, can you tell us what it refers to?'

Susan picked up the card and started to read the verse.

> *This Capricorn Was Smart*
> *She Was Having A Ball*
> *But She Was Found Wanting*
> *When Death Came To Call*
> *Although She Never Gave Up*
> *She Fought With Her All*
> *But It's Always A Good Day*
> *When Geminis Fall*

Susan finished reading the verse and put the card back on the table.

'Does it ring any bells with you?'

'No, I'm sorry, it means absolutely nothing to me,' said Susan.

'The only thing that this poem and Wendy have in common is that her birth sign was Capricorn, other than that it doesn't make any sense at all.'

'Any idea what the reference to the last two lines, particularly the last line, "When Geminis Fall", can you think of anything?' asked Pete.

'No nothing,' sobbed Susan, 'believe me, those words mean absolutely nothing to me'

If there was one good thing that Pete possessed as a cop, it was his ability to recognise the expressions of an honest answer and Susan had just passed the test.

'Is it possible that she was seeing somebody, possibly somebody that she didn't want you to know about?' Max asked. 'Maybe someone, that for some reason because of your friendship, she couldn't tell you about?'

Max was hoping his probing questions might unsettle Susan, enough for her to share one of their secrets with the two detectives.

'You mean like..., having a physical relationship with some guy, like... having an affair?' I...eh... I don't think so!' blurted Susan, 'we may have acted a little flamboyant in our approach to men, we possibly flaunted ourselves a little at times, but we drew the line when it came to the marriage cheats. You could pick those guys out from a mile away, the seedy grubby type with the pale coloured circle on a finger, caused by a missing wedding band, a definite giveaway. Wendy wasn't in any relationship, and if she was, she would have told me so, in fact, I know she would have told me so..., we shared all our secrets.'

'And what kind of secrets did you girls share?' Max asked.

'Oh just women's stuff detective, our hopes, our dreams, our aspirations on how we were both going to change the world.

'Detective Hammond, should I be worried...!? Do you think I'm in danger, is Wendy's killer going to target me...?' Susan asked, the tears still running down her cheeks.

Max reached across the desk, his hand squeezing her petite little fingers in an effort to console her.

'No, absolutely not!!' he answered, hoping his quick response was a sign of assurance to Susan. 'In fact I would say you are probably the safest woman in New York city at the moment.

'Besides,' quipped Pete, 'you've got the best two cops in New York watching your back!'

'Thank you,' said Susan, a little visible smile showing across her face.

'Okay, I'd say we're pretty much done for now,' said Pete, 'we have your contact details if we need to talk to you again.'

Max closed the door after Susan had left and looked across the room at Pete.

'Well, what do you think, he asked?'

'She's telling the truth, she knows nothing, you can hear it in her voice and those tears were certainly not crocodile tears! At the moment boss… it looks like we have nothing to go on…'

'Okay, let's give her an hour, then you call her, arrange to meet her at Wendy's apartment first thing in the morning, go over it with a fine toothcomb, you know the drill Pete, no stones unturned, get Susan to check through Wendy's facebook page for the last day or two, also any other social media platforms that she may have engaged on, and when you're done with that I want you to check out what life insurance policies she held, did she have any investments in other properties, shares, bonds, anything. I want to examine the branches of the family tree, a list of living relatives, if any, I want to know of anybody that might benefit from her death.'

'Jesus, that's going to take up a lot of my time, Max,' said Pete.

'Yes it is…, and when you finish doing that, I want you to check with prison records, find out if any high profile rapists, wife beaters or women haters have been released in the past six months, if there are, I want names, addresses, I want to know where they're hanging out, particularly those living in and around New York City.'

'I have a bad feeling about this one Pete,' said Max, his eyes gazing down on the killer's calling card 'he either knew her or he knew of her, there's a connection somewhere and we need to find it, and we need to find it fast!'

'Do you think he's a local.?' Pete asked.

'Maybe, when you look at the surrounding landscape, the ease of access to the spot where Wendy's body was found, there's no doubt our killer was familiar with the area, he knew exactly where he was going to dump the body, even before he killed her, let's wait and see what the forensic report from the lab tells us tomorrow!'

26

February

The dark clouds gathering on the horizon would surely bring rain, thought Max as he looked skywards, a strong gale blowing in from the west swept past his face as a ship's foghorn blared in the distance, interrupting his thoughts. Max didn't like the rain for two reasons, one, it could very easily contaminate a crime scene, washing away vital forensic evidence and two, it accelerated the arthritic pain to his knees and hips, resulting in excruciating agony for hours, sometimes days. There was a time when he could examine a crime scene crawling around on all fours, now he could barely crouch over a dead body, often struggling to get back on his two feet without help.

He had over the years, made several appointments with his doctor, some which he kept, and some which he did not. He even took the time to visit a herbalist who sold him some magic herb potions. Nowadays, he felt that every wince that shot through his body was a form of payback for not looking after himself. He knew that if he didn't do something about it soon, he could very well end up a cripple.

Like every crime scene that Max had worked on, he would scan the first twenty feet circling the victim before actually studying the body, this was so familiar to the murder of Wendy Carlisle, late twenties, possibly early thirties, brunette, dressed casually, but you could tell her attire was certainly not cheap.

She wore an expensive leather jacket, a cherry layered blouse, regular fitting black pants and red shoes. The top two buttons of the blouse were noticeably missing, most likely torn off and lost in the fight to survive, The injuries to the upper part of her face and head were severe, She had obviously been beaten with a stick or a club, however, the abrasions and marks around her neck and throat would suggest that just like Wendy Carlisle, she died from asphyxiation. However, unlike Wendy, who had shown all the hallmarks of a determined struggle to survive, there were no signs of the same on this victim. There were no visible defensive wounds, no cuts, bruises or abrasions on her hands, arms or legs. There were no lacerations on her wrists to suggest that she had been tied up like Wendy, absolutely no evidence that even remotely suggested that this young woman had tried to defend herself in any way from her killer.

Judging by the sparsity of congealed blood spots at the scene, it was obvious that the killer had struck elsewhere, possibly one or two days ago, the body then transported to this location for it to be found. Again, it bore all the hallmarks of a serial killer, her jewellery untouched, expensive earrings, a gold cross and chain around her neck, two eye catching diamond rings rested neatly on the middle finger of her right hand while her black designer bag lay by her side, the contents inside the bag included her wallet, cash and her all in one cosmetic make up pack, there was no evidence to suggest that the victim was sexually assaulted, the autopsy would determine whether she was or not, one thing was certain, robbery was not the motive.

'Do you think we're looking at the same guy who murdered Wendy Carlisle?' asked Pete, showing a concerned tone in that gravel voice box of his, his dark grey gaberdine, matching the colour of the clouds passing above his head.

'Yeah, it's the same guy all right!' Max answered, 'look around you Pete, it may not be the same location where Wendy Carlisle's body was found, but the surrounding landscape is almost identical, a popular pathway, very little lighting, the body's not hidden and again, it's close to a levee. Plus, he's left his calling card again!!'

'On Wendy Carlisle's body we found the Capricorn sign of the Zodiac with a poetic verse attached. The Capricorn star sign as we know, is in around the months of December and January, Wendy's birthday was January ninth correct?'

'Yeah somewhere around that' said Pete, 'can't specifically

remember the exact date, but knowing you, it's correct!'

'Now we have a second body with another calling card, except the Zodiac sign is Aquarius, and we also have a second verse. You can bet your bottom dollar that this victim's birthday falls sometime this month or early March.

Who found the body?'

'The guy over there smoking the cigarette,' answered Pete.

'Says he was out walking his dog when he came across the body, the dog's barking drew his attention to the area where the body was. He's pretty shook up and who can blame him.'

'Has anything been touched or moved?'

'No I don't think so, with the exception of the dog, as far as I am aware, the body has not been contaminated in any way, I've been in touch with the SS team, they're on their way.'

'Good, Pete..., can you get one or two of those uniformed guys to cordon off the area, say a thirty metre radius with the "Do not cross" tape. I don't want to facilitate any of our media friends in having multiple orgasms over this!'

Max hated the media, he always likened them to a gaggle of geese, especially the lowlifes who scampered around day and night, following the death trail, smelling the blood, hoping that they would get the scoop that would put their shit news reporting on the front page. He had an aversion to their methods of investigative journalism, they showed no respect for the victims or their families. He couldn't understand why they would pursue their underhand line of enquiries, digging up the past history of innocent siblings, dramatising the lives of others, for a couple of bucks. Then again, were they any worse than the MSM journalists who were in the Governments pockets, failing to report on the real issues of health and homeless policies that were being inflicted on the American people. In the old days, journalists could be trusted, it was a time of give and take, with reliable sources on a level playing field, no such thing as fake news. Nowadays, for journalism, it was a race to the bottom, it wasn't even about headlines any more, it was about how many likes you got on social media, it wasn't even about the truth any more, it was about click-bait and how many people agreed with you whether you were right or wrong. Social media was now the pariah of mainstream journalism, journalists were now competing against each other while their ethical badge of honour was diminishing with every passing day.

Max had covered a lot of crimes over the years, seen a lot of bad things done to people, but this was different, somehow his gut feeling was telling him that this was going to be the biggest challenge of his career.

'Keep an eye on those crime scene investigators, Pete, I don't want them touching the body until forensics get here, also, it looks like somebody's been doing a bit of fly-tipping, there's a couple of black garbage bags thrown into the bushes on the far side of that clump of trees, get one of the young officers to go through them with a fine toothcomb, not sure whether we'll find anything of interest, but let's start by ruling out the obvious, in the meantime, I'll go flash my shiny badge and have a chat with our smoker before the skies do finally burst open, the way my knee's are acting up right now, it won't surprise me if we get the thunder and lightning as well!!'

27

March

Jenny O' Brien knocked gently on Max Hammond's door and stepped inside his office, her large frame casting a shadow that dominated almost half the room. She could tell when the lieutenant was in a pensive mood and half regretted stepping into his office in the first place. Although Max had always shown Jenny the respect that she deserved, she was petrified of her boss. She saw him as the sergeant major of the precinct, the one guy you didn't get on the wrong side of. Maybe he reminded her of her father. Max looked up from his desk as Jenny quietly shut the door behind her.

'This better be good Jenny, what is it?' Max asked, already knowing from the worried expression on her chubby face that it was not going to be good news. Jenny continued to stand by the door looking at Max in a hesitant pose.

'C'mon Jenny, out with it, I haven't got all day!'

'Well Sir,' Jenny said, nervously puckering her lips, 'there are two issues, and I think they may be related. A young woman's body has been found in the Buttermilk Falls area, early reports say the body was found in a secluded area and there is a printed card stapled to the lapel of the victim's jacket.'

'*Holy fuck!!*' shouted Max as he leapt from his chair, grabbing both his jacket and the holster which housed his 9mm Glock.

'Jenny get in touch with Forensics, tell them to get to the crime scene pronto, but tell them nobody is to touch the victim until I get there, is that clear!! what's the second thing you wanted to say to me?'

'Well Sir, there was a couple waiting at the front desk, husband and wife, they have reported their daughter as missing.'

'Fuck, are they still here?' asked Max.

'Yes Sir, I've put them in one of the holding rooms down the hall.'

'Good, I'll go talk to them straight away, what are their names?' asked Max as he raced down the hallway.

'Albert and Monica Hoffman and they're in interview room number 2' shouted Jenny, raising the tone of her voice, not sure whether the detective had heard a single word she said.

Before Max entered the interview room, he stopped to clear his head, to control his breathing and appear calm. He already had two murdered women in the morgue and he knew in his gut that this number was going to rise. Max entered the room and introduced himself to the Hoffman's.

Even though he was sitting down with his clenched fists resting on the edge of the table, Max could tell immediately that Albert Hoffman was a tall man, well over six foot. He was smartly dressed in an expensive pin striped suit, light blue shirt, a dark blue tie, held neatly together by a silver tie bracelet with silver cuff links to match, while the wedding ring on his "ring finger" boasted of a lot of carats. No shortage of money here, he thought to himself. Monica Hoffman on the other hand, looked as if the clothes she was wearing were just picked up off the floor. Max could tell she was wrought with anxiety, she looked haggard, exhausted, and probably hadn't eaten or slept, for a couple of days.

One could sense that the thick layer of blusher which was applied to her cheekbones was more to do with camouflaging the stress of the last few days rather than a professional cosmetic makeover.

'Desk Sergeant O'Brien tells me you think that your daughter may have gone missing, why would you think that, Mrs Hoffman?'

'Her name is Charlotte,' answered the distraught Mrs Hoffman, although she spoke eloquently, her nervous tone and demeanour suggested that this was without doubt, her first time ever inside a police precinct.

'She's twenty eight years old and we haven't heard anything from her since Friday,' said Mrs Hoffman, biting hard on her lower lip, the water noticeably welling up in her eyes.

'She was to come around for dinner on Sunday like she usually did, but she never arrived at the house, and now we're concerned that there may be a connection between the recent murders and our daughter's disappearance.'

'Did Charlotte have a boyfriend? was she in a relationship?' asked Max.

'No, not to our knowledge, she had had a few boyfriends over the years but nothing serious or long term, she was very particular when it came to relationships. She was a good clean living girl, in fact the only thing that she had done that we considered uncharacteristic of her upbringing, was that about six months ago she had a tattoo, a "badass tattoo" is what she called it, etched on the upper part of her leg, other than that, we were both proud of the way she had turned out, weren't we Albert...?'

Albert Hoffman just nodded in agreement, the blank eyes embedded in his freckled forehead continuing to stare at the desk in front of him. Max felt that it was like he wasn't even in the room, but at the same time, was eavesdropping on every word that was spoken by his wife.

'And what was this "Badass Tattoo?" a dragon? a snake? can you give us a description?' Max asked.

'It was a tattoo of a dark red rose that crawled up the outside of her left thigh, almost shooting to the hip.' answered Mrs Hoffman, clearly embarrassed but not judgemental of her daughter's promiscuity in the unashamed surrendering of her body, exposing her naked thigh to a complete stranger.

'When was the last time you saw or spoke to Charlotte?' asked Max.

'I last spoke to her on Friday afternoon.'

'What time?'

'About four pm'

'And what exactly did she say.? Did she say anything that you would have thought was out of the ordinary.?'

'No she seemed very jolly in herself, was rambling on about some cute guy that she had met a couple of days earlier.'

'Did she say whether she met him in person or online, a dating agency perhaps…?'

'She never said, I assumed it was in person.'

'And did she put a name to this cute guy, even perhaps a first name, Mrs Hoffman?'

'No she did not, but…, she did say he was one hell of a catch!
And that's the last we heard of her, no contact whatsoever since, and it's driving us insane!!

'I assume you have tried to contact her by mobile?,

'Yes we have, but either the battery has run low or it's been switched off completely. We've been to her apartment twice, but there are no clues as to where she might have went, and her car is parked in her allocated space outside the apartment block, so she can't have travelled far.'
'Well maybe she's with this cute guy right now, maybe she's not in a position to recharge her phone, Charlotte could pop up at your front door at any time.
What about her close friends, have you tried contacting them? you know kids these days, they tend to forget their parent's still worry about them, even if they are twenty eight years old' said Max, trying to reassure the mother as best he could, even though his gut feeling was that very shortly he would be investigating a murder scene, and the body of their daughter Charlotte, would be the focus of his investigation.

'Lieutenant, I have photographs of Charlotte on my phone that I can show you...' and as Mrs Hoffman reached into her bag for her phone, Max put his hand out to stop her.

'Mr and Mrs Hoffman, I appreciate this is a worrying time for you both, and I want to assure you that your daughter's safety is utmost in my mind, but I have to be in a really important place right now, so I am going to hand you back over to the desk Sergeant. Jenny will take all the necessary details from you both, however I have one question to ask before I go, it may seem like a strange one but believe me it's an important one!'

'What question is that?' asked Albert Hoffman, who up to now had contributed absolutely nothing except an irritating noisy belch every couple of minutes.

It was the first time he had spoken during the interview.

'What question is so important in relation to our daughter's whereabouts?'

Max looked at both parents, 'What is your daughter's date of birth and what is her birth sign?'

Mrs Hoffman looked deeply into the detective's eyes as she spoke, 'It's March twelve, 1987 and she's a Pisces!'

Max let go of Mrs Hoffman's hand and pushed himself back into the wooden chair.

'Mr and Mrs Hoffman, I want to be perfectly candid with you both, I urgently need to go right now, like I said, Sergeant O' Brien will be in to talk to you both in a couple of minutes, thank you for your time.'

Max left the room and headed for the exit door, his head in a spin, nothing could convince him otherwise that the killer had struck again and the dead woman found up in Buttermilk Falls was indeed Charlotte Hoffman!

As Max sped out through the police precinct gates he speed dialled Pete's number on his mobile.

'Hey Pete, we have ourselves a third victim, on the way to the crime scene now!'

'Yeah I heard,' answered Pete, 'from what I hear it sounds like our guy all right, I'll see you there in about fifteen minutes.' Max switched on the police car siren and headed for Buttermilk Falls on the outskirts of Manhattan.

Over the years, when interviewing parents or couples, Max was always quick to figure out which one of the couple was the domineering one in the relationship, but the Hoffman's were a different class, they gave nothing away, there were no interruptions, no talking across or shouting down to each other. Albert came across as one of those genteel individuals, it was like he had given his wife a free pass to speak for both of them. Max put it down to the respect that both parents had for each other. On any other day, thought Max, with parents like Albert and Monica, Charlotte Hoffman would have been a very lucky girl, however, today was not going to be that day.

By the time Max arrived at the crime scene, the Forensic people were already there, some of them on their hands and knees, sifting through twigs and gold coloured leaves. Although he had given instructions that nobody was to touch the body until he arrived, Sharon was already bent over the corpse, camera in hand, taking pictures, particularly of the young woman's exposed left thigh.

'You found the rose then,' said Max, the blood draining from his face, disappointed, evened saddened that it was indeed Charlotte Hoffman and he was now dreading the thought that it was he who would now have to break the bad news to her dear sweet mother.

'Yes, how did you know...?' Sharon asked.

'I've just been talking to the parents down at the station, her name is Charlotte Hoffman, she was supposed to call to her parents for Sunday dinner but never showed up. Her date of birth is March 12th, 1987 and guess what!? she's a Pisces.'

'Yes, I know,' said Sharon, pushing the calling card into his hand. For now Max was only interested in the last two lines of the verse and the killer did not disappoint him.

"But It's Always a Good Day,
When Geminis Fall"

Max, walked around the crime scene, careful not to contaminate possible evidence, but he knew there would be no evidence, absolutely nothing, the killer would have made sure of that. Max, did however, open a gold locket that was worn around the neck of the victim. Inside was a picture of Charlotte and her mother smiling, cheek to cheek in happier times. This was the third murder committed by the same killer in the last three months and each of the three crime scenes were almost identical, and yet the killer hadn't made a single error.

Even though Max took all his cases personal, this one probably affected him the most, a beautiful loving family torn apart. For the Hoffman's, their only child, who they had watched over and protected for so many years, had been taken from them, taken without warning and brutally murdered, her body then dumped in some dirty woodland grave by a deranged sadistic killer. As he drove back to the city, his main thoughts were how he was going to break the news to the Hoffman's, how was he going to tell them that their baby girl was dead.

Throughout his career, Max Hammond had come face to face with some of the most evil people in America, but this was a new low, even for him, he contemplated throwing in the towel, get a cushy job somewhere, maybe become a Private Investigator, a profession that by all accounts was a very lucrative business to be in at the moment, but as soon as that thought came into his head, he dismissed it just as quickly.

This fucker was not going to better him, this fucking animal was not going to beat him, he vowed to himself that he would drag the killer, kicking and screaming to the tabernacle of justice, dead or alive, one way or another…!

He owed it to the victim's families, he owed it to Charlotte, but particularly to Monica Hoffman and her husband Albert. There was something about the Hoffman's that opened his eyes, that had got him thinking about life, about love and how fickle our hopes and dreams become when you lose a loved one.

28

'Christ Max...!! you stink of booze,' Pete said, 'when was the last time you were in contact with a bar of soap or a toothbrush? You smell like a two week old dead cat.

You do realise that we have a meeting with McKenzie at twelve sharp. It's now nine thirty,... why don't you go home, take a shower, have a shave, change your clothes and get back here for eleven thirty. If anything comes up in the meantime..., I'll cover for you, actually Max..., and I'm speaking as a friend, it might do no harm if you stayed off the booze for a while, at least until we solve this case, until we put this bastard behind bars. Now go on, skip off home and Max..., be sure to use plenty of deodorant as well.'

'I wonder is that guy losing the plot?' Pete thought to himself as Max closed the office door behind him on the way out. He had been introduced to Max about fifteen years ago and had been his partner for the last five. During those five years he had learnt a lot from the master, how to read a crime scene, search for the motive, put yourself in the position of the victim, try and visualise the circumstances that would have occurred before the crime, and when you had accepted yourself as the victim, you changed sides, you then delved into the mind of the killer to understand his way of thinking, what was his purpose? what was his motive?

What was the killer going to gain or achieve by carrying out this evil act. Was it to do with love, hate, jealousy, possibly aided and abetted by a full moon, a lunar sway perhaps, or maybe just a random robbery that had gone wrong. Once you forensically examined the crime scene, figured out the motive, you would understand the killer and the jigsaw pieces would practically join together themselves, piece by piece to complete the overall picture. Max had such an easy way of doing things, he was the perfect module for any budding young detective, but Pete was now questioning whether his boss was buckling under the pressure.

Over the past couple of weeks, he had noticed a change in Max's personality, it was a slow change but a change nonetheless, the black circles were starting to appear under his eyes, you could tell he wasn't getting much sleep, and he was losing weight, eating less than normal and in particular his drinking habits had changed. He was now drinking on a daily basis and it was clearly affecting his work ethic. Maybe he was becoming obsessed with our killer, maybe it was the lack of clues, the lack of evidence that was getting to him. The last thing he needed now was a lecture from the Chief, reprimanding him, telling him how to do his job.

The fact that they had made no arrests so far didn't help and Pete knew McKenzie was going to bring that up at the meeting. Explaining to McKenzie, that Max was a total egalitarian, a man of high morals and principles, a man who would not arrest a guy just to appease his boss's or the media, would not sit well with the chief and Pete knew it.

Pete rose to his feet and walked across to the filing cabinet, he searched through the files and walked back to his desk throwing three brown folders onto the hard surfaced desktop before sitting back down again. He sat in silence for a couple of minutes, scratching the top of his balding head, searching for answers while staring at the three manilla files on his desk, the one on top belonged to Wendy Carlisle, the middle one belonging to Mandy Duncan and Charlotte Hoffman's file lay on the bottom.

He picked up Wendy's file for what seemed like the hundredth time in three months, scrimmaging through page after page scrutinizing all the evidence before him, painstakingly going over every line, every paragraph of every statement that they had taken from witnesses at the bar, paying particular attention to Susan's statement, looking for that something that would give them the breakthrough so badly needed in this case, that little something that would be screaming at you from the page, but you would be unable to sense it, unable to see it.

Pete scanned the photographs of Wendy's corpse and the

adjoining crime scene with a magnifying glass, 'Come on Wendy, tell us something, show us something, anything that will help catch your killer, help us nail the bastard that did this to you.' Pete had the same conversation with Mandy and Charlotte and was just closing the files when Max walked through the door, a cup of coffee in each hand.

'Well fuck me!' Pete said, 'What a difference an hour and a cheap bar of soap can make, who would have thought that such a transformation could be possible in such a short period of time. You should be on one of those reality TV shows where they transform people from one extreme to the other!'

Max looked a different cop, clean shaven, clean suit, fuck..., he even managed to smell good.

'Did I miss anything?' Max asked as he passed a piping hot cappuccino to Pete,

'Any new leads, anything at all?'

'No Max, nothing, absolutely nothing' answered Pete, who was not afraid to show his frustration and disappointment at what he had just said.

'Okay, let's go see the Chief, it's not going to be a teddy bears picnic so let's get it over with!'

The two detectives entered McKenzie's office together and both sat on the hard wooden chairs that were waiting for them. Chief Philip McKenzie sat opposite both men, you could sense that he was going to be on the offensive, his hands were clasped firmly together and he looked inquisitively into the eyes of his two detectives.

Max had made a habit of avoiding eye contact as much as he could with his boss, not because he was afraid of him or because he was his superior, but McKenzie had this huge conk that seemed to stretch out for miles, and Max knew that if he looked at it for too long, he would break out in a fit of laughter.

Sharon had always said that if Pinocchio was a real kid, a DNA sample would have proved beyond doubt, that McKenzie was the father.

However, if Max was old school, then McKenzie was old old school, he had aged a lot over the years and Max reckoned he was somewhere north of fifty and was now just biding his time, waiting for the opportune moment to bow out, a generous golden handshake, a nice juicy fat pension that would be more than adequate to see him live out his remaining years in comfort.

Over the years, the Chief had proven to be an excellent police officer and had worked his ass off while slowly climbing, or as others called it, leapfrogging up the senior officers ladder, avoiding the slippery snakes along the way. He was a good leader, and had the respect of not just his subordinates, but had also made a good impression on his peers as the photographs and plaques, which were beginning to overcrowd his desk and cabinet would suggest. During his unblemished career, McKenzie had been promoted to Captain in his early forties and had so far avoided any internal or external scandals, not a shrink or hint of evidence of accepting bribes, profiteering, nothing, zilch! he was as clean as a whistle!

By the time he had been appointed Chief, he had started to slow down, his personality changed, maybe it was his age, but he was now concentrating his talents on reducing crime statistics, whilst also reducing the yearly administration budget of the department.

McKenzie soaked up pressure like a dry sponge soaks up water in a small lake, and had always managed to avoid confrontation with his superior's. Experience had taught him to run with the hare and hunt with the hounds, always an opportunist when it came to the good news photoshoots but, when the shit hit the fan, he always kept his distance, sat on the fence and was always willing to say the right thing to keep everybody happy and onside.

But today was different, he didn't come across as a happy bunny at all, and the daily tabloids that were strewn around the desks, showing recent photos of three murdered girls didn't help the cause of the two detectives in the room.

'See this ear, detectives,' growled McKenzie pointing at his right ear, 'do you know why it looks a lot rosier than the other one? Well let me tell you why... let me enlighten both of you of how my morning has gone so far. I've just got off the phone from the Mayor's office and believe me guys, he ain't happy, not one little bit, he wants to know why this department hasn't handled things very well with the press, he wants to know why we haven't made one arrest in relation to these homicides and how some dumb fuck in my department has leaked this Zodiac shit to the press, and guess what…? the press now want to know are we going to have a dead body every month for the next nine months!!?'

'The Mayor has in no uncertain terms let me know that he wants results on these homicides pretty soon, his term of office is up at the end of the year and the last thing he needs is a shit storm of murders and astrologers crawling around his office at election time. He has made it quite clear, considering I had to tell him that we don't have a suspect, not even one…, that he will not entertain failure, and the last thing I need is that cunt of a Mayor swarming all over my ass for the next couple of months.

Theres a lot of anxious people out there, so when we've finished our meeting and you guys leave my office, the first thing I want you both to do, is take off those fucking blinkers that you're wearing, go out there and shake a few trees, make a couple of arrests. Hammer it home to your investigative team that I want to see results, and I want to see them asap. I want this office to be seen to emphasize, particularly to the women of New York City that they are safe! Maybe then one of you guy's can provide me with the answers that I can pass on to his Lordship so…, which one of you is going to make my day just that a little bit easier, hmm…, oh, and one more thing, I want you to put a muzzle on your team, from here on in, nobody speaks to the press without my consent, are we clear!'

Some days McKenzie could come across as an endearing asshole, castigating all before him, and today was turning out to be one of those days. Max took hold of the reins, hoping to defuse any heated exchanges before they got out of hand and leaned across McKenzie's desk.,

'Chief, you know me, I have been harassing and chasing crooks all my life, it's what I crave, it's what I live for, I could fob you off right now, I can spew you out a whole bunch of lies, fabricated shit that I've just made up, just so that you and the Mayor will sleep a little easier tonight, however, I'm not going to do that!

At this moment, outside of the killer's calling card, we have very little to go on, nothing circumstantial, our killer is smart, he doesn't leave any clues and as of now, we haven't even established a motive. Nobody has reported anything out of the ordinary, nobody has reported anybody behaving suspiciously, we don't even have a suspect!

Our friends in forensics tell us that the three girls were murdered by the same killer a couple of weeks apart, and we know that if we don't catch him soon he's going to kill again, sometime in the next two weeks to be exact!'

'How do you know that? how can you be sure?' asked McKenzie.

'Well sir, the killer has left his calling card on all three victims. Even though all three victims were entirely separate individuals, had nothing in common with each other, his "Modus Operandi" was the same.

'His first victim Wendy Carlisle was a Capricorn, born on January 9th and we believe the killer knew that even though they had no connection, they had never met before the night in question.'

'So how did he know?' asked McKenzie,

'Well Chief, Pete and I believe he had his calling card with him when they met, the killer was prepared, he knew how the night was going to end. At the moment we haven't figured out how he manages to do that, it's like the guy is a ghost, he's invisible, he's left us nothing to go on and we haven't been able to make the connection yet.'

'And what about the other two girls?' asked McKenzie.

'Nothing Chief, again stalemate, the only thing that connects all three girls are the calling cards that the killer leaves behind.'

'What about Forensics? Have they made any connection between the victims, have they offered any suggestions in relations to the killings.?'

'Nothing, they're as baffled as we are, like I said Chief, the only connection is the calling cards, Wendy Carlisle, born in January, under the star sign Capricorn, Mandy Duncan, born in February under the star sign Aquarius and our latest victim, Charlotte Hoffman born in March under the star sign Pisces. That's why I believe his next victim will be born under the birth sign of Aries, born between March 20th and April 20th so, if we take it that the killer is consistent, and my hunch is correct, the killer won't strike again until sometime between those two dates, which by the way gives us some sort of a buffer, plus, thanks to forensics, we know that Wendy, Mandy and Charlotte were killed either on the Friday night or the Saturday of those weekends. I think it's fair to assume that the killer will strike on the following dates.'

Max opened his brown folder and handed Pete and the Chief an A4 sheet with the following typed on it:

Friday March 22nd, Saturday March 23rd.

Friday March 29th, Saturday March 30th.

Friday April 5th, Saturday April 6th.

Friday April 12th Saturday April 13th.

'How can you be sure of this?' asked McKenzie.

'I can't… but it's the only hunch I've got Chief, it seems logical from what we are looking at, that the killer will strike again sometime between those dates, it's the consistencies of the killings so far, it's like having a habit. If I'm correct it means our man is killing his way through the birth signs of the Zodiac, selecting his victim's by their birth dates, we need to figure out how the killer knows their birth signs, how does he track them down, possibly through a dating agency or dating App, plus the fact that he has his calling card with him on the night, so he must have a connection in some way with the girls before he meets and murders them.

'Our killer doesn't just walk into a bar or stop someone on the sidewalk and says 'Hey babe, my name is John Smith, what's yours…? Oh, and by the way what's your birth sign? You could be up and down the bar or street all night. No, this guy is clever, he has settled on his prey at an early stage, he's done his homework and he's prepared. The question then is where do they go after they leave the bars, it's obvious that he takes them somewhere, a house, a building, perhaps an office where he works and then kills them, no sexual assaults, robbery is not a motive, he just kills them. He then places the bodies in locations where there is easy accessibility to the public, He knows the areas are popular with dog owner's, joggers, places where he knows they will be found quickly, he wants the bodies to be found, he wants us to collect his calling cards, the question is … *why?*'

What's also consistent is that all three girls were found a couple of minutes walking distance from a lake, which would suggest that he first transports the bodies by boat, carries them onto dry land, to a place which I believe he has already selected and lays them on the ground, yet nobody has seen anything, nobody recalls anyone acting suspicious, it's like he's invisible!

'However, the real question is, what's his motivation? his purpose for these type of killings? What's he hoping to achieve…?'

You know something Chief, you know what really bothers me…? It's the last two lines of the verse on his calling card,

"But it's always a good day,
When Geminis Fall"

'Although the calling cards found on the three victims were for different birth signs, the last two lines on all three cards are the same, what's he making reference to? what's he trying to tell us? What's the connection with the star sign Gemini?'

'Chief, you mentioned that the press are asking are we going to have a Zodiac victim every month, the answer is no, I believe our Ghost will stop after the Gemini murder!'

'Why do you think that?'

'The three cards reference the Gemini twins, he's talking plural here, however the twins were half-brothers so maybe he's only going after one of them and if he succeeds and we still have no solid leads to go on, it's possible that he'll stop, and if he does…, there is the chance that we lose him forever!'

29

Max Hammond sat back into his old leather chair, both hands pressed against the back of his head, his long legs sprawled across the desk in front of him. He looked up at the calendar on the far wall even though he knew the date would not have changed since he had looked at it an hour earlier, yes it was still Thursday, April 18th and the clock on the wall at the front desk said it was 8.30 am. With the exception of a fracas at the front desk a couple of hours earlier, it was strangely quiet inside the station at that time of the morning. Rather than going home the night before he had opted to stay in his office overnight, catching a couple of hours sleep before his investigating team were due to arrive. He hadn't been this early for work in a long long time. For the past couple of years, his Wednesday nights would have been spent in one of the many bars that would have invitingly embraced him on the way home to his one bedroom apartment.

Last night should have been the same, but it wasn't…, there was a killer on the loose and Max was convinced that between tomorrow Friday and Saturday he would kill again. Maybe the killer would be out there tonight thought Max, lurking in the shadows, stalking his prey, like a leopard stalks a deer or a gazelle, checking the direction of the wind, calculating the angle of the strike, the element of surprise after the isolated prey had become detached from the herd.

On the white graphite board opposite from where he was sitting, Max looked at the photographs of the three girls that he and Pete had pinned up a couple of days earlier. Also on the board were photographs of the crime scenes which showed the areas where the bodies were carefully placed in easy accessible areas, so that they would be discovered early. There were also blown up copies of the killer's calling cards, and their sinister encrypted messages. When Max checked the clock again it was 8.55 am and as he looked out through the dust covered white blinds of his office window, he could see the troops starting to congregate in the main briefing area, quietly chatting with each other.

They all had obviously received the internal memo the night before. He had worked on and off with most of these guys over the years, they were good cops, officers of the law that you would trust with your back, cops that you could depend on. He allows his thoughts to go back a couple of years, reminiscing on the good old days when they would all meet up in Mike's bar after their shift had finished. They would shoot some eight ball, take the piss, play pranks on each other, particularly on the younger inexperienced guys and most nights would be guaranteed to finish with a sing song. For some reason that he couldn't now remember, he had deliberately ostracised himself from the motley crew, preferring to go solo. Perhaps, it had got to the stage where, when it came to calling a round at the bar, all the other guys were lagging behind, not because they were slow getting to the bar but the fact that they were drinking sensibly. Or perhaps it was around the time his relationship with Sharon had hit choppy waters and was about to capsize with neither of them wearing a life jacket. Sometimes he would look at Pete with envy, envious of the fact that he was an excellent detective, had built a solid marriage with Shelley and a proud father to three great kids, epitomizing the just reward for lifes efforts. Whatever the reasons, now was not the time or the place to contemplate on the past, life's earlier failures or misdemeanours should not disqualify him from facing up to the biggest challenge of his career. 'Just might have time to get another coffee before we begin,' he thought to himself, heading straight for the coffee machine which was conveniently located at the top end of the hallway.

Fresh coffee in hand, Max took a long deep breath and walked into the open area, looking and nodding at each of his officer's. He could feel the buzz in the room, a reminder to him as to why he loved getting the nod for these tough assignments. Max took a sip from his coffee before addressing the investigating team standing before him.

126

'Okay people listen up, I want your full attention for the next twenty minutes or so, which also means that I want all mobile phones switched off until the briefing is over.

Because of the horrific nature of these crimes and the media interest that they have generated, the Chief has seen fit to invite a criminologist, a profiler to the case. Her name and proper title is, Professor Maria Sanchez, and she should be joining us in a few minutes, I want you all to be cordial and courteous towards her, make her feel welcome, give her as much support as you can.'

In reality, Max didn't have much time for these so called criminal profilers, but having said that, he recalls he didn't have much time for DNA when it was first unveiled back in the seventies and seen as a major breakthrough in forensic science.

Max had a lot of collars on his CV, including five convicted killers, two who were doing life with no chance of parole and there were three on death row who would gladly swap their sentence for life without parole.

Max was a great believer in ground work policing, always following the murder trail, sniffing out the clues that the killer would without doubt leave behind, but most of all he believed in gut instinct and would go to extraordinary lengths to get a result, however, because these heinous crimes had all the trademarks of a serial killer, and according to the chief, the professor had proven herself to be exemplary in this type of criminal behaviour, he welcomed as much help and cooperation he could get. Plus it was either the Professor or the Chief in his face, and so opted for the lesser of the two evils.

'Okay, let's get started shall we? let's take it from the top!

'Victim number one, Wendy Carlisle aged thirty, an only child, whose parents are deceased, she lived in an apartment in Queens, worked as a real estate agent, and a pretty successful one by all accounts, On Friday January 11th she leaves work at the usual time, and from what we know, all the appointment slots in her diary for that week were ticked off, she then goes to the Bootlegger's Bar on 21st Street in Queens to meet up with her close friend, Susan Carter, an electronics engineer.

According to Ms. Carter's statement, we know that with the exception of annual summer vacations, Christmas, Easter, that sort of thing, they have met there every Friday for the past two years, spending a couple of hours together, having a few drinks, discussing the week gone by, some girlie talk, whatever that means? and then went their separate ways until they would meet up again the following week, except, on Friday January 11th because of work commitments, Ms Carter never showed at the bar.'

'Although we never found Wendy's phone, Susan's mobile records tell us that they had a two minute conversation that evening. We also know from witnesses in the bar that Wendy was there from around six pm onwards, one of the bartenders recalls seeing her there, speaking to a couple of the regular guys but to one guy in particular who was definitely not a regular.

'Did the bartender give a description of the guy?' asked Herb,

'Yes he did, described him as male caucasian, over six foot tall, dark hair, well dressed, probably somewhere between late forties, early fifties.'

'What about CCTV in and around the bar?' asked Charley.

'Well here's the thing' answered Pete, who had now joined Max close to the white board.

'According to the bar manager, there wasn't any, the CCTV cameras were down for a couple of hours that night, said they were having trouble with the security equipment over the Christmas.'

'Their security guy put it down to the bad snow we've been having for the past few months. Apparently snow and ice can cause havoc with the exterior fibre network...?'

'Want me to follow up on it Boss?' asked Herb,

'I worked as part of a surveillance team for over two years, I know a bit about cameras, recordings n' stuff like that, maybe I can have a chat with this security guy, rattle his cage a little bit...'

'Yeah you do that Herb, just make sure you also note the dates and times that the other blips occurred, who knows there may be a connection there, also when you get the relevant information, check with the Met office, find out what the weather conditions were like on those dates. I'm not convinced one bit that the freezing weather was the cause of those blips and speaking of connections…, I really do believe that these girls knew their killer, they may have only known him briefly, maybe it was just textual stuff on a dating site, a short meet over a casual drink perhaps…, but there's no doubt about it, there had been a connection of some sort with him prior to the night they died!' One thing is certain…, their killer already knew them!'

'Isn't it unusual boss?' asked Bob Newton, 'the fact that the victim's money and credit cards, were still on their person when they were found.'

'Yes and no', answered Max. 'Credit cards and ATM cards are not as popular to thieves as they used to be, too many cameras on street corners these days and practically every ATM has at least one camera looking down at you. I remember, years ago, making an arrest in one of the big financial institutions in Manhattan. One of their employee's had stolen another employee's wallet. When the employee reported the wallet stolen to his bank, they were able to tell him that three hundred dollars was taken from his account just an hour earlier from an ATM that was actually located in the building, obviously it was the thief that took the money and he was identified on camera by the companies security personnel.'

'But how did he know the pin number?' asked Bob.

'It was easy, the day before, the thief had been in the queue at the ATM, the other employee was in front of him and as he tapped in his pin number, the thief could be seen looking over his shoulder and then writing down the number after he had gone. The thief knew that the other employee kept his wallet in his desk drawer and stole it during lunch hour. The point I'm making is, that these days your average thieves, burglars, pickpockets, all prefer to steal cash, to them cash is king, you can spend it anywhere, whereas all cards transactions can be traced no matter where they are used.'

'But this isn't your average mugging boss,' said Bob, 'we're talking murder here and not even a cent is taken!'

'Yes, you're right again Bob, and this is why we should be worried,' answered Max.

'Given that our victim's are female, I want you to check did any of the girls use the same hairstylist, visit the same beauty parlours, nail technicians. I appreciate all these suggestions are long-shots guys, but somewhere out there, someone knows something, there's a connection, we need to find that connection and find it fast!

All three girls suffered horrific injuries, we now know from our friends in pathology that none of them were sexually assaulted, so our killer isn't interested in sex and we also know he's not short of a few bucks, so why is he doing it...? what's the purpose of his killings? What's his motive...? anybody...??'

'He could be killing just because he likes to' answered Bill Frazier, 'he's a psycho, he doesn't need motive, he doesn't have to have a purpose.'

'What about his calling cards Bill?' asked Pete. 'He's playing mind games, he's telling us something, he's leading us somewhere..., this guy certainly has motive, he has an agenda, and he's killing to justify an end result and we need to figure it out pretty soon!'

'Forensics tell us that from dust particles found on the victim's shoes, it's more than likely all victims were killed in the same place, then he transports them to their already chosen burial place, how?, we don't know yet, by car, van, possibly even by boat, to a place he knows where the bodies are sure to be found.

I've asked the chief to instruct all precincts to increase uniform numbers on the beat and also to increase checkpoints around the perimeters of Queens and Manhattan, particularly after 10 pm.

And of course there are his calling cards, copies of which you can see on the board in front of you, the cards are stapled on to the right lapel of each victim's jacket.

'Each card carries a star sign, a birth sign, call it what you want, but each sign is connected to the birth date of the victim, so far we have Wendy a Capricorn, Mandy, an Aquarius and Charlotte a Pisces, all cards carry a different verse relating to the victim's birth sign, but what is significant is that all the verses finish with the same two lines, 'But it's always a good day, when Geminis fall'

'What's the link? to be honest, we don't know, Pete and I have racked our brains over this for the past couple of months without success, we can't exactly pinpoint what exactly the killer is telling us.'

Max's briefing was interrupted when Sharon entered the room accompanied by a young attractive woman, probably in her middle twenties. Sharon introduced her as Professor Maria Sanchez, a criminal profiler from the D.A.'s office.

'Professor Sanchez, welcome to the team!' said Max as the professor entered the room.

'You come highly recommended, maybe you can make sense of all of this, hopefully, with your experience you can create for us a profile of the killer and give us something positive to work on?

'Well, my feet haven't quite touched the ground yet Lieutenant, and obviously I haven't had the opportunity to study these case's in a more professional manner, but from the information Professor Stillman has supplied me with and from what I have observed as a neutral over the past couple of months I would say the killer possesses an IQ of at least 120, he is a man of means, he's confident, especially when it comes to seducing young women, has huge belief in his ability to kill, but what's most important for him, is the self belief that he will not be caught.

His arrogance would suggest that he has killed before, possibly a couple of years ago, and was never caught. Maybe in some weird unexplained way, by killing again, he is now cleansing his soul of a previous killing spree. At the moment as I look at the board, I do not understand what the messages mean or what the killer is referring to, but it's blatantly obvious that our killer doesn't like women very much, in fact he despises them and there is no doubt he will continue to kill.'

'Professor,' interrupted Pete, 'would you say our killer is one of those people who goes around listening to the funny little voices in his head, is it possible he possesses an alter ego, perhaps thinking that he is carrying out God's work on earth?'

'Absolutely not, these women didn't harm anybody, they had no police records, no criminal convictions, if there was a slur on their combined past, they had Charlotte Hoffman to thank for that, she was issued with a parking ticket just over two years ago, which I might add, was paid on time. To the best of our knowledge they were good decent people. What we know for sure is that they were not kidnapped or forced to leave the bars with him, they left with him of their own volition, he knows how to charm the ladies and win them over. They weren't gullible people, they felt confident and safe in his company, never once considering that they might be in danger. They wanted him badly, so badly that they threw caution to the wind, professional women who just dropped their guard and ended up on a cold slab in the morgue...'

'Could he be posing as a gigolo Professor?' Herb asked.

'That's a good question, but the answer is no! firstly the profiles of the three victims would suggest otherwise, and secondly, our killer clearly has an agenda. Gigolo's are normally supplied by an agency and are not generally handpicked by their clients, whereas our three victim's were undoubtedly handpicked by their killer. None of these killings were carried out impetuously, every thread, every strand of each killing was meticulously woven.

'The fact that there were no signs of sexual activity, consented or otherwise, is it possible that our killer is impotent? asked Mike.

'No, I don't think he has any sexual deficiencies, there is no evidence to suggest otherwise, which begs another question..., why doesn't he have sex with them!!?

The opportunity was there, they were all attractive women who left the bars with him, fully believing that there was going to be sex, there was no doubt about that.'

The three encrypted messages so far would suggest that not only does he like to boast about his killings, he likes to be in control. He's dominant, but not overbearing, he's using his charm and possibly his wealth as the tools to draw these women in, he manipulates them so easily, they fall under his spell without realising it, it's like he hypnotizes them, I would suggest that his charming ways are his main accessory for murder.'

'And what's the basis of that rational, Professor?' Pete asked, gesturing the Professor to expand on her evaluation of the killer's profile.

'Up to now, he has lured three mature intelligent women to their deaths, he didn't manage that with his wealth alone, you can have all the money in the world, but if you're born an asshole, you're also most likely to die an asshole, all the money in the world won't change that, however, if you are born with a charming dispensation and a nice smile, then the Gods have been kind and have given you a head start in life, now…, if you are born with both those gifts, then you are born with a twenty four carat flower of magnetism, the world and beyond is your oyster!! The down side is there is a danger that you can become a megalomaniac, that you convince yourself that you are more powerful than anybody else. The fact that he keeps referring to the Gemini star sign, the birth sign of the twins might suggest a couple of things. Come the month of June, he has already targeted a set of twins as his prey, however if we were to look at the flip side, maybe our serial killer is not working alone, maybe he has an accomplice?

'How can we be sure that there are not two killers at large, two brothers perhaps, or two half brothers like Castor and Pollux!'

'At the moment, I'm just speculating, just throwing it out there, that someone else could also be implicated in these murders, however, give me until the morning to study the case files and hopefully I will have some answers for you.

'One other thing,' added Professor Sanchez, 'there is no doubt in my mind that we have at least one serial killer on the loose, roaming freely across the streets of New York City, one of the reports earlier, likened our killer to a ghost, so let's start playing with his ego a little, let's make him feel that he is untouchable, immortal.

'What would you suggest Professor?' asked Max.

'Let's give him a name, let's give him an identity, he'll like that, and who knows, we might get a response. We could just call him "The Ghost of New York" or perhaps we could personalise him with someone that lived in… Dickensian times, someone like Silas or Jacob, I'm sure he'd like that, the fact that we are recognising, acknowledging his prowess, his skill's, however… the one thing that we do need to make sure of, is that his name doesn't roll off the tongue like a Gacey, a Bundy or a Dahmer!'

'Okay guys, you all know the drill, at the minute we are assuming that the victims only connection with each other is that they were killed by the same person. Herb, you go check the pub's CCTV, Jeff, go back and talk to the parents and relatives of the three girls, extract as much information from them as to their daughters previous history, employment, social life, habits etcetera, for the past five years, talk to their old bosses and friends, like I said we have to be absolutely certain that the only connection that exists between these women is that they were murdered by the same person.

Bill, go back on old unsolved files, say for the past five years, see if you can dig anything up, have a look at old paper clippings, stuff like that, who knows, we may get lucky!

Just one more thing, the Chief has made it very clear that some of the people over in City Hall are not happy with the way this investigation is being managed, they reckon we're not kicking our heels hard enough so let's make sure that we make them eat their words!'

Max showed the professor into his office and pulled a chair towards the desk, gesturing for her to sit down.

'Thanks again for your assistance in this case Professor, while you're here, feel free to use my office for your case studies, the files belonging to the three girl's are on the desk. Perhaps we can do an evaluation on them first thing tomorrow morning!

The professor nodded her head in agreement.

'How long do we have you for Professor?' Max asked.

'I've been directed to stay as long as it takes, lieutenant, hopefully I won't be in your hair for too long.'

'Just one other thing, Professor, there was a suggestion that we set up a confidential hotline specifically in relation to the murders, maybe there are people out there who might possibly know something but are afraid to call in case their identity is revealed.

What do you think?'

'Not a good idea right now, speaking from experience, over ninety percent of calls to a police hotline are just crank calls that waste precious police resources and can also shift the focus from the real evidence to hand, also I can guarantee you that if we were to set up a hotline right now, by this time tomorrow you will have at least twenty people claiming responsibility for the murders.'

'That's exactly what I was thinking Professor, I just wanted to hear it from you, it's important to know we're reading off the same page.'

'Yes it is Lieutenant ... however, I would suggest allocating at least one person, possibly your desk sergeant to keep an eye on the social media aspect of the murders, get her to trawl through some of the content that could be relevant, who knows, if we make this personal, our killer might be tempted to get involved in one way or another.'

Max nodded his head in agreement as he pulled the door shut and left the office.

'Pete... you come with me!!'

'Where are we going?' Pete asked as he jumped from his desk and ran down the hallway in pursuit of his boss who seemed to have an extra pep in his step today.

'Well, we know that the killer did his homework on his victim's, he knew everything about them before he met them that's for sure, now we need to do the same with him, we do our homework on him and with a bit of luck we will nab the bastard before he kills again. The Gemini sign has me worried, if we don't catch this guy by June and let's say he kills a set of twins, what if he just stops killing after that? what if he disappears, disappears without trace, having achieved what he had set out to do in the first place, what if our Ghost just vanishes into thin air? immortalised forever!

You heard what the Professor said, it's possible that this guy started killing years ago, then stopped, now something has triggered him off again and we don't know if and when this guy is going to stop, I have a list of all the trendy bars within a three mile radius of where the girls were last seen alive, you and I are going to check them all out, see if any of the bar staff recognise any of the girls, after that we go visit the top ten dating agencies in New York of which I also have a list of, the killer knew their age, date of birth, where they hung out on the weekends, if one of the agencies has one of our girls on their database, then it is very possible that they will have a file on our killer as well.'

'Jesus, it's gonna be a long day Max,' quipped Pete, as he threw the stub of his cigarette on the pavement, crushing the burning ash into the ground with the sole of his shoe.

'It sure is my friend, but right now I'm famished, I need to eat and that's why I'm going to let you buy me a good old fashioned breakfast before we start!'

'Oh, and by the way, get the word out to the rest of the team, from now on we refer to him as Silas, our ghost, we're going to call him Silas!'

'Brilliant,' Pete thought to himself, 'looks like the boss is back to his old self again!'

30

It was Monday morning and the clock had just struck nine when Natalie Johnson stepped into the elevator that would bring her to her office on the twentieth floor of the ame**RK**omm building. She was in an upbeat mood for a Monday morning, part of her weekend had been spent with her son Joshua on an exiting fun filled trip to the city Zoo. Josh was four years old and like any other kid of that age, the trip to the City Zoo would be the highlight of his week. Natalie sat into her desk and switched on her computer, her eyes moving around the enclosed office which was surrounded on the outside, by an open plan system. Employees were busy taking up their positions at their desks, pressing buttons, bringing their laptops to life, each employee starting the new week, overflowing with good intentions.

Natalie loved her office, although stuck away in the corner of the twentieth floor of the high rise building, it was compensated by a spectacular view of the east side of the Hudson River.

She would begin her week with the daily ritual of watering the bunch of Begonia flowers that blossomed sweetly in the flower pot on the right hand side of her desk, she would then kiss the oak framed photograph of herself and Josh, taken in Disney World just before Christmas.

On the far wall, hung a picture of Natalie with her parents, celebrating her tenth birthday party and on one of her filing cabinets stood a crystal glass vase, two thorny red roses protruding from its mouth. The two roses were a memory of her parents who were now deceased. As the clock ticked by, Natalie, apart from having a quick coffee, had been so caught up in her work that when she eventually looked up at the clock, it was 1.10 pm.

She normally went to the company canteen at 1pm, but today she was running a little behind on her work and needed to close a project that she had been working hard on, she reckoned another five minutes should do it.

Just as Natalie was heading to the canteen, she heard a voice cry out,

'FUCK!! FUCK!! FUCK!'

With a puzzled look on her face, she scanned the open planned offices to see if she could see anybody, but the office floor appeared to be empty. As usual, curiosity got the better of Natalie Johnson, and she walked across the open plan floor, slowly glancing from left to right, until eventually she was able to pinpoint where the vocal outbursts were coming from.

She considered calling security when the voice then yelled out…

'Well fuck it anyway!! why the hell did I take on this job in the first place?'

The voice was coming from a lone partitioned cubicle close to the coffee vending machine. Natalie silently tip-toed towards the cubicle which had gone silent again and peeped over the top, only to see a guy on his knees, head in his hands, and completely entangled in multi- coloured wires and cables, which were scattered all over the floor.

'Hi there' said Natalie in a low pitched voice, trying not to scare the guy. 'Are you okay? can I help you in any way?'

Startled, the young guy looked up, feeling a bit embarrassed with the situation that he found himself in.

'Oh sorry Miss, I didn't realise there were still people working on the floor, I was told that everyone would be gone to lunch between one and two and it was the best time to get this job done.'

Natalie looked at his ID badge,

'So tell me Mr Daniel Montgomery, what are you trying to do? – blow up the building!!?'

'No Miss, nothing as simple as that, I work for the IT maintenance section of the company and I'm trying to hook up all the computer systems onto the one server, something to do with time and motion. Apparently once this is hooked up, the company can see just how much time you work, and how much time you actually spend surfing the social network scene, and as you can see,' both his hands pointing down at the entangled cables, 'I'm not doing a very good job of it! Did you ever have a day when you get up in the morning, full of hope and ambition for the day ahead, and something just gets in the way, it's then you realise that you have got out of the wrong side of the bed, and to make matters worse..., I got a speeding ticket on the way over here this morning, never rains when it pours, isn't that what they say.? By the way, don't tell anybody about the time and motion thing, if that gets back to my boss I could get the sack!

'Don't worry, my lips are sealed. You know what? said Natalie, 'why don't you take a break, leave it for now and come back later, you might have a different view on things when you get back. I'm just on my way to the canteen, why don't you join me? my treat!'

'Why not?' Danny said.

'How come you don't carry ID on you, what's your name?' Danny asked.

'It's Natalie, Natalie Johnson and yes you're right, I'm not carrying ID, but, when your Uncle owns the building, you kinda get away with not wearing a badge all the time.'

'Wow, you're fucking kidding me!! you mean you're Ross Kingsley's niece, fuck I got to watch my language..., shit..., there I go again, you know what..., I'll just shut my mouth completely' Danny said, feeling embarrassed with himself for the second time in as many minutes. Natalie on the other hand found it funny and laughed out loud. They walked together to the elevator that would take them to the company restaurant on the 28th floor. As the elevator climbed the building, floor by floor, Danny being cautious with his words this time, began to speak.

'Wow I can't believe that I'm going to lunch with the niece of Ross Kingsley, that guy is regarded as one of the greatest American heroes, a living legend. I was only six years old at the time, but I remember seeing him on the TV, he was mesmerising to watch, so brave. What's he like when he takes off the mask and the cape, is he normal? does he eat? does he even sleep?'

'Of course he eats and sleeps,' laughed Natalie, he's just a normal guy, but he is everything that people believe and say about him, he's like a father to me, my parents died when I was young and he has taken care of me ever since.'

'Oh, I'm sorry to hear about your parents, how did they die.?'

'My mother and my aunt were killed when the terrorists flew the planes into the Towers, they were both in the South Tower at the time of the attacks, my father took it very hard, so hard he committed suicide shortly after. One night he went out to the garage, hooked up a hose to the exhaust pipe of his car, locked the windows and doors, turned the ignition on and went to sleep.

He was found by one of the garbage guys the following morning. The garbage had not been put out the night before so the garbage guy opened the garage door and found my father dead in the driver's seat.'

'Oh my God that's terrible! Did he leave you a note saying why he did it?'

'No nothing, I know he loved my mother very much, I know he missed her and longed for her every minute of every day, but he always promised me that he would look after me and protect me as long as he lived. To this day I still try to understand why he left me on my own, maybe it was just too much for him in the end.'

'Anyway..., let's talk about something else, what about you Danny boy? what's your story?

'Tell me something about you, with a name like that you have got to have Irish blood running through those biceps...,' asked Natalie as her heart skipped a beat for the second time in as many minutes.

'Well I know my great Grandfather was one hundred per cent Irish when he disembarked from a boat in Boston Harbour to make his fortune many years ago, can't say whether he made his fortune or not though, if he did, maybe I wouldn't be cross wiring cables for a living.

My parents still live in Boston and I go visit them a couple of times a year. I share an apartment with two other guys just on the outskirts of Manhattan, living the dream you could say!'

'What about girlfriends?' asked Natalie, her heart again skipping a beat.

'No nothing serious' replied Danny, 'what about you Natalie? what's your story? you married? you got kids?'

'Yes, I was married, got married young, I have a little boy, Joshua, whose now four years old. My marriage didn't work out so I got divorced. I live over in Staten Island now, got my own apartment, doing just fine!'

'So…, is that a good story or a bad story?' asked Danny.

'All depends how you look at it, I went through a hard time, but I'm happy now, my ex-husband was a violent and aggressive man who became very difficult to live with, so for the safety of my son and myself I divorced him, Uncle Ross took it upon himself to cover all the divorce costs and set me up with my own apartment in Staten Island. The irony of it is that my mother was a very successful divorce lawyer but I don't think she would have got the settlement that he got! I have full custody of my son and that's all that matters.

It's funny how your life can be turned on its head, and without my Uncle Ross, things could have turned out a lot worse for me and Josh… so yeah, I guess uncle Ross is my great American hero!' Danny looked at his watch and was surprised how fast the time had gone, 'Hey Natalie, thanks so much for the lunch and I really would love to talk to you some more, but I've got to get back to my work, I only get a thirty minute break, if I go over that I've got a boss who loves to remind me that he's the guy in charge, so thanks again for lunch, really enjoyed your company,' and as he headed towards the restaurant exit door, Natalie called out after him,

'Hey Danny, fancy a pizza and a beer after work?'

'Yeah…, why not, where do you want to meet up?' Danny asked.

'Tell you what Danny Montgomery, why don't you give me a shout when you pass my office around 5.30 this evening.'

'Okay, see you then' Danny said, giving a thumbs up and a smile as he headed for the elevator. Natalie watched Danny as he walked along the glass windowed corridor, not quiet sure why she had just done that. She had never been that upfront with a guy before, maybe it was time to shake off those divorce blues, perhaps it was time to start enjoying life again.

Natalie couldn't believe that she was contemplating such notions while at the same time questioning how and why your heart skips a beat when you meet someone for the first time? what was that unexplained feeling, that flutter she had never experienced before, maybe it was his Irish charm that had her heart telling her something, was this the start of a new love for her? a new life for herself and Josh? only time would tell!

31

It was a cloudy grey Saturday morning and a light drizzle was falling from the skies above. Max used a half worn chamois cloth to wipe clear the condensation and moisture that had pooled together on the front and back windscreens of his car. He then checked that he had put the miniature little flask in the glove compartment, it didn't matter how much coffee was in the flask, Max always allowed room for about three shots of bourbon. He preferred his coffee black, the occasional shot of bourbon compensated for the lack of milk but added greatly to the flavour, plus it was hard to detect the smell of bourbon on your breath, particularly if it was five parts coffee. Before he embarked on the eighty mile journey to Sharon's house, he reminded himself to stop at a gas station on the way and buy some flowers for her. His way of saying thanks for meeting him on her day off.

Max had to turn the ignition three times before the car's pistons jumped into life. As he drove towards the Interstate 86 highway, he began to prepare his opening gambit for when he arrived at the house. He had phoned Sharon the evening before and they had spoken at length about the homicides, she had agreed for him to call on the Saturday morning adding, the only stipulation was that when he called, he would leave his gun in the car.

Over the years, Sharon had seen and experienced first hand the damage caused by gunshot wounds, hence her dislike for firearms. She couldn't understand the logic of how an eighteen year old could legally purchase a semi-automatic, yet would have to wait another three years before he could walk into a liquor store to buy himself a beer.

Max did not manage much sleep himself and was showered and dressed by 7am. For the next hour, in between drinking black coffee, he packed all the evidence that had been gathered by the homicide team into boxes and put them into the trunk of his car. Although she showered at least once a day in the workplace, Sharon looked on those as wash-downs as opposed to taking a shower and enjoying it. For her there was nothing more soothing than having a shower first thing in the morning, letting the hot water run for a couple of minutes before stepping inside the steamed up glass cubicle, the experience of the warm water cascading downwards like a waterfall, her whole body awakening, the torrent of droplets crashing down on her neck, forming into little ripples that flowed downwards in all directions, invigorating her senses. Sharon had just stepped out of the shower and donned her bathrobe, when she heard what she thought was gunfire, gunfire that was getting louder and nearer every couple of seconds. It was only when the doorbell rang that she realised what the racket was. It was that familiar sound you get from a nineteen ninety eight sedan when the exhaust that should have been replaced a couple of years ago, is still clinging on for dear life. When Sharon opened the front door she could only giggle, Max was standing on her doorstep, completely concealed, trying his best to juggle the boxes to prevent them from falling.

'Good morning Max, you do realise that I asked you not to call too early, I guess some of those old habits never change', she said, as she took one of the boxes while gesturing him to follow her through the hallway and into the old antiquated living room which was situated at the back of the house.

The interior decor of the house hadn't changed much since he had last visited, the same wallpaper covered the walls, most of the furniture still positioned in the same place, in fact the only thing that had seem to embrace change over the years was the lightly coloured yellow cornice moulding that ran across the walls close to the ceiling which he remembered was originally white when he and Sharon's father had put it up. Max always liked that room, the antique furniture, the framed paintings on the walls, most of them oil portraits, the black and white photographs in their old wooden frames neatly placed on top of a writing bureau. Max walked across to the far side of the room and picked up a framed photograph which was familiar to him. It was a photograph of Sharon, her parents Bob and Martha, and Max, enjoying a day out on Liberty Island.

'I see you still look after your mother's bonsai babies!' said Max, pointing to the Japanese Maple and Chinese Elm trees on the window sill over on the far side of the room, while at the same time kicking himself for forgetting to buy the flowers on the journey up.

'Yes I am,' answered Sharon, 'although I didn't have the time to look after all of them, those two were Mum's favourites, so I kept on to them, one of each in memory of Mum and Dad. The rest I dropped off at one of the charity stalls in a nearby shopping mall, I'm sure they found good homes eventually.'

For Max, the nostalgic return to the house brought back the memories, both good and bad. At the beginning of their relationship, he used to call on a regular basis. He had gelled well with Bob, while her mother Martha, who always baked him her special flapjacks, was the finicky type, always fussing over him whenever he called. Over a period of time, Max had formed the impression that because she was an only daughter, her parents who were devout Catholics would have approved of them getting married, but it was never to be.

Both her parents had since died. Bob, who was a diabetic, had been bedridden for over two years after suffering a stroke, spending nine months in a home before he died, while Martha, who was housebound, outlived her husband by just a couple of months. With the benefit of hindsight, Max acknowledged that he should have been more comforting, more supportive of Sharon's feelings when she needed him most, instead he began to focus more on his job, immersing himself in his work, while ignoring the needs of the woman he loved and it bit deeply into their relationship. Maybe, thought Max, that was the tipping point of their relationship and the love and respect they had for each other from that point began to fade, diminishing slowly until the flickering light went out and there was nothing left to ignite.

Eventually, after they had split up, Sharon moved back into the house and quickly settled into her own routine. Max knew that he was still in love with her, and would probably love her until the day he died. It hurt him deeply that she did not feel the same, but accepted that he had only himself to blame. She had come into his life, enriched his heart and soul and he had pushed her away. It was now clear to Max that whatever bond, whatever understanding they both had in their mutual quest for justice, when it came to their personal relationship, it was totally incompatible.

'Put the boxes on the couch Max,' shouted Sharon, startling him back to reality, 'as you can see, I too have been busy, I've cleared the table so we can lay out the photographs of the victims, the crime scenes can go here on the desk bureau, the calling cards and whatever else you may have to hand can fit on the coffee table.'

'So, first things first, do you want some coffee or would you like me to make you breakfast? You look like you've lost some weight over the past couple of weeks, how have you been eating lately?' asked Sharon as she walked towards the kitchen, conscious of the fact that she may have pressed a nuclear button in his head without thinking through the consequences of her question.

However, Max did not comment on his weight loss, nor did he answer her questions regarding his eating habits.

'I'm the cop,' he thought to himself, 'I'm the guy who gets to ask the questions and make the observations.'

'Coffee's just fine thanks, black,' he answered as he emptied the contents of the boxes, one by one onto the allocated spaces, some falling on the polished sandalwood floor as he did so. He quickly separated everything, placing the victims photos on the left hand side of the table, crime scenes in the middle and the killer's calling cards on the right hand side.

The forensic reports and his laptop, he put on the couch for later analysis.

Sharon returned to the room with a roasting pot of coffee, and two mugs which she placed on the little bit of space that was left on the small oak coffee table. They pulled their chairs closer to the table and sipped on the hot coffee as they both slowly examined the evidence in front of them.

'It's a long time since I've seen you out of a suit, Max' said Sharon, commenting on his dress sense, a stylish lumberjack shirt with the two buttons opened, a stonewashed pair of denim jeans and a navy pair of moccasin slip-on shoes, all he was missing was the cowboy hat and he could have passed off as an oil baron from Texas.

'You know this is going to take time Sharon, are you okay with this?' he asked.

'Of course I'm okay with it, believe me, if I wasn't, I wouldn't have agreed to meet with you on my day off, so let's get started, shall we!?'

'Okay, but just before we do, before we get into the nitty-gritty stuff, I've got a question for you…, what's your professional opinion of Professor Sanchez…?'

32

'Why Max, do you fancy her? To be honest, I can see why you would, she's a very attractive woman' said Sharon, smiling to herself.

'C'mon Sharon..., you know what I mean, I just thought she came across as a bit of a drama queen, having these preconceived notions about twins and the possibility of more than one killer, I think she's making a lot more out of something that's a lot less!'

'And what if she's *not*?'

Max didn't answer.

'Do you know she drives a crimson coloured convertable?' Sharon asked, knowing full well that her off the cuff remark would piss him off, just a little...

'*What!!* You're fucking kidding me,' snapped Max.

'What professional person, particularly a professor, travels to work in a convertible for fuck's sake!!?'

'What's wrong with it? Is it because she's a woman, Max!!?

'Ah c'mon Sharon, let's be serious, a profiler that drives a convertible, one surely contradicts the other!? You were there yesterday when she addressed the team, these people speak in a different language to the rest of us, do you think her profile of the killer is accurate? it's clearly obvious we have a serial killer on the loose, but her theory that there may be two killers, even a set of killer twins on the loose, I just don't buy that at all..., that's one of the reasons I phoned you last night, you asked me earlier was I eating okay, well the truth is I'm not! I can't eat, I can't sleep, in fact for the past couple of days, all I've done is drink coffee with whiskey, whiskey with coffee, and it's saturating and clogging up my brain cells..., that's why I need your help Sharon, I'm banking on your expert opinion, your experience as a pathologist, I'm hoping that by the time we sift through what's on the table in front of us, one of these girls will have reached out to us, telling us why they were chosen, telling us why they had to die.'

'Let's give the Professor a chance Max,' answered Sharon.

'You may have found her a bit drab, perhaps a little boring by your standards, but I thought she gave an excellent introductory speech, she took a methodical approach on the few facts that she had at her disposal and whether you like it or not, you can't disagree with a lot of what she said, she wasn't afraid to speak her mind in front of the team and she has a warm charming charisma about her. Personally..., I like her. I thought she was forthright in her assessment of what we know so far, giving a balanced insight into the mind of our killer while setting the tone for what we may be dealing with over the next couple of months. I believe the professor's profiling techniques could be a valuable acquisition to your ongoing investigations, so whatever you do Max, don't piss her off, do not baulk or dismiss any of her methods or suggestions until you think them through.

If there were any signs of dissension in the room yesterday, they were coming from you!!'

'What!' I thought I was very cordial towards her, I made her feel welcome, I may not have had her wrapped in cotton wool but I did give her the freedom of my office, fuck, I even gave her a chair to herself!'

'I'm just saying Max, I would rather have her on my team than pitching for the opposition.'

'What do you mean by that!?' snapped Max.

'I got a call from an old friend of mine in the bureau last night,' answered Sharon, 'he was showing an interest in the investigation, asking questions about you.'

'What kind of questions?'

'Questions about your ability, your leadership, whether you had the backing of the team working on the investigation, wanted to know were you up to it...?'

'And what did you tell him?'

'The truth!'

'Which was?'

'Firstly, I questioned why the reputation of a detective of your calibre was in disrepute.?

He said something about directives coming from the Mayor's office, said the rumour out there was that you were suffering from fatigue…, that you were all burned out!'

'And what about you Sharon? do you think I'm burned out.?'

'Don't worry Max, I told him that the most experienced cop in New York City was on the case and was making huge progress towards closing out the investigation. I'm just letting you know that the FBI are taking an interest in "Silas", so make sure you work within the rules Max, don't give them any reason or encouragement to steal your case from under you.'

'The FBI using a Machiavellian approach to steal my case, who would have thought it?' said Max shaking his head sarcastically.

'It's not funny Max, do you understand what I'm saying.?'

'Yes, I understand, now let's get to work!!'

33

'The killer uses the same M. O. for all his victims,' Max said, 'no trace of drugs, just alcohol, and plenty of it, very little traces of food which means that whatever about the killer, the victims wouldn't have eaten since probably lunch time. Again the killer knows the movements, the habits of his victims prior to meeting them for the first time, and after filling them with alcohol, they go somewhere with him, of their own free will, where he kills them, I know you said there was no trace of drugs in their bloods, but could he have used something like chloroform, a substance that would only stay in the body for a couple of hours?'

'It's possible,' answered Sharon, 'but unlikely, depending on the amount used, some of the side effects of chloroform are nausea and vomiting, none of the girls showed symptoms of either, so I'm positive we can rule it out.'

'Wendy is the key person in all of this, she was killed on the Saturday while Mandy and Charlotte were killed on the Friday. She was the only one to fight back, she was the only one that he did not have control over while she was alive. Even your pathology report suggested that she freed herself by placing food in and around the nylon tie-wraps. She almost escaped, only to be caught again by her killer.

For the next eight hours, the detective and the pathologist sifted through all the evidence and the medical reports without success, they were still no closer to identifying the killer, and the pathologist appeared more frustrated than the detective.

'Max, I don't know about you but I'm feeling quite ravenous, it's time to order in some food, do you still eat that Chinese dish, Kung Pao chicken?'

'I haven't eaten it for awhile,' said Max, 'but because it's you asking, and I'm too tired to argue, I won't refuse!'

Dusk was starting to set in, the setting sun resting on the outer limits of the New York skyline, creating a colourful panoramic view that shepherd's would delight in. Sharon had most of the evidence packed neatly back in the boxes when the doorbell rang. The food had finally arrived and was a welcomed distraction from their workload. They both sat on the floor, relishing their Chinese cuisine. Sharon sipped on a red claret that had been breathing for over an hour while Max opted for a regular cold beer. The classical music that played softly in the background, added greatly to the ambience in the room. They sat for over an hour reminiscing on old times, both of them laughing at the good times, while pondering on how they could have changed or altered the bad times. It had been a pleasant evening, for Max it was a welcome distraction from what he would have been doing if he had been on his own. Deep down, he stilled loved Sharon, she possessed this alluring trait that one fell in love with almost immediately, unfortunately for him, he just never knew how to express his feelings into words, if he had, things might have been so very different.

After a spell of silence between them, Max spoke. 'Sharon, there is one more thing that I want to run by you, I decided to leave it until last because I didn't want it to influence or have a bearing on what we've already looked at today, I didn't want it to impact on your professional rationale until we had exhausted all other avenues. Last Thursday night, I went back to the Bootlegger's bar and parked my car in the parking lot situated at the back of the building, however to access the parking lot, you have to drive down a narrow street at the side of the bar. After parking the car, I then had two options to enter the bar. I could walk through the smoking room at the back of the building, or I could go back out the way I came in, walk back up the side street and enter through the main entrance at the front. For the simple reason that I don't smoke, I opted for the latter, walked around and entered the building from the front. The bar itself was quiet, probably twenty, maybe twenty five people scattered around the place, talking, laughing, some sitting on their own, their heads stuck in their phones, minding their own business.

I just sat at the bar and had a beer, spent some time talking to the bar staff and questioned some of the regulars. Would you believe, one of the regulars I bumped into, was a guy I arrested for a car felony about fifteen years ago.'

'Surprised you remembered him after that amount of time.'

'I knew straight away it was him, the guy has a very prominent cleft lip, plus he has a speech impediment as well.'

'Is he a suspect?'

'No, he's harmless..., his passion is stealing cars, not killing women. One of the barmen who sported a neatly trimmed goatee, suggested that I call back on a weekend night, remarking that the Monday to Thursday crowd were geriatrics compared to the weekend warriors, a different bunch altogether, a much younger, vibrant and more energetic crowd, who excelled in letting their hair down after a hard week's work. Other than that, I didn't learn anything that I didn't know already, so I left. However..., when I left the bar and walked back down the side street heading back to my car, something caught my eye at the far end of the car lot. There's a wall about six foot high and on the other side of that wall there's a street running parallel to it.

'So?' asked Sharon.

'Well, there's a fishing tackle shop on that street which has security cameras fixed above the shop front. It was too late to do anything about it on Thursday night so, yesterday morning I popped in to introduce myself to the owner, a guy called Sam Warring, he was in the middle of a break, coffee in one hand and half a hot dog in the other, and given the amount of ketchup and mustard that took up half his chin, it looked like he was enjoying it immensely, probably enjoyed plenty of hot dogs over the years, given the huge pressure his shirt buttons were under around the midriff but..., the sight of all that still didn't stop me from introducing myself.

'Nice guy, Mr Warring, one hundred percent New Yorker, even though you wouldn't think it at first.'

'Why not?' asked Sharon.

'Well, he's got these beady eyes, narrow slanted ones, like those guys over in Chinatown, to be honest, I half expected he was going to answer me in mandarin when I asked his name.

Looking at all the gear on display in the shop and given the fact that I'm left handed, I asked him whether there were different type fishing rods for us left handed people, say…, just like golfers.

'And is there?'

'I don't know!'

'He didn't answer the question…, well he did and he didn't, what he said was, with fishing reels, left is right and right is wrong!'

'What does that mean? asked a puzzled Sharon.

'That's exactly what I asked him!'

'And what did he say?'

'He said, well you're the cop, go figure!'

Sharon laughed quietly to herself, making a mental note, that at some later stage she would call in on Mr Warring, and thank him personally for making her smile and brightening her evening.

'Anyway, all jokes aside, he's got a fabulous shop, he's got all these fishing rods lined up against one part of the shop, a huge selection of fishing reels, different colours, different styles, all encased inside a glass counter top, it was like being in a gun shop!

Sharon…, did you know that a really good fishing rod can set you back around five thousand dollars!? and if you take in all the accessory gear, like waders, fishing hooks, gut and a nice hat, the whole thing could set a landlubber like me back about ten thousand bucks, a lot of money to spend on yourself just to sit in a boat for hours, pondering to yourself if a little fishy fishy is going to make your day.'

'Maybe you should take up fishing,' said Sharon, again displaying that cute smile all over her face,

'it might help you to relax, take your mind off things for awhile.'

'Take my mind off things for a while!' Max said, laughing out loud.

'Sharon, in case you hadn't realised, guys like me go fishing everyday, we exist in a large pond, it's called New York City, where the little fish, the minnows are gobbled up by the bigger fish, the low life predators who lurk at the bottom of that very pond, the great whites, the red bellied piranhas, the slippery eels who kill without hesitation or remorse, just because they can. That's when I do my fishing Sharon, every day I bait my hook and sling it into the dark murky waters of New York City, then I sit in my little boat and wait, catching a predator can take time, but if you sit patiently knowing that you have used the right bait, the great whites, the red lions, the slippery eels will bite, and that's when you reel the bastards in, slowly but surely, hook, line and sinker!'

'Well thanks for that informative analogy Max, very interesting indeed,' quipped Sharon.

Max was still deep in thought, every waking day was a new challenge for him, no matter how hard he worked, no matter how many criminals he put away, it would not bring an end to the crimes or the violence, the horrific way in which humans treated other humans, there would be no cessation, not even a brief one. For Max, the quest would never end.

'So tell me, were they working?'

'Were what working?' asked Max, confused as he quickly jumped back to reality.

'The security cameras, were they working? and if they were, did Mr Warring keep copies?'

'Yes they were, and yes he did! He keeps them for six months, something to do with the terms and conditions of his insurance, in fact I have copies of December, January and February right here' Max said, waving the three compact discs in the air, grinning from ear to ear, like a little boy who had just received everything that he had asked for from Santa on Christmas day.

Max opened up his laptop with the intention of inserting the discs when Sharon burst into laughter.

'What's so funny?' he asked.

'I'm sorry Max,' chuckled Sharon,

'It's your screen saver, "The Keystone Cops" it's just hilarious, surely you could have put something more appropriate to your work!'

'But it is appropriate to my work Sharon, it reminds me of the way things used to be down at the precinct before I joined.

'Would never have put you down as a conceited old git Max' said Sharon, still amused by the screen saver on the laptop..

Max inserted the January disc into his laptop and clicked onto the January 9th icon.

Because of the positioning of one of the cameras on the fishing tackle shop's wall, it also covered a small area of the bar's car lot. Max scrolled forward to approximately 8.30pm and pressed play.

Although the car lot lighting wasn't great, the recording quality was good, however because some overhead shutters were partially blocking the view, it was hard to get an overall picture of the car lot or the people going in and out of the bar, but depending on what direction you walked across the lot and depending how tall you were, it was possible for that one camera to record an image.

Max continued to play the recording for a couple of minutes and then pressed the pause button.

'Did you see them?' He asked excitingly, 'did you see them...?'

'Did I see who?' asked Sharon, shrugging her shoulders.

'You didn't see them? Okay, let's play it again and this time keep a close eye on the top right hand corner of the screen.'

Max scrolled back the footage and pressed the play button again, while Sharon concentrated on the top right hand side of the screen,

'Look!! do you see them now?'

Sharon's vision was now focused on two people walking towards the far side of the car lot and getting into a car.

Although it was dark, Sharon could just about make out the back of the woman and part of her head, but because of the man's height you could only see him from the shoulders down. He was a muscular guy, solid build, confirming Max's assumption first day that the killer was strong, fit and well able to carry his victims to the selected locations.

'Can you zoom in closer?' Sharon asked.

'Yeah,' Max said, as he scrolled the button enlarging the image on the screen.

'Fuck…, *IT'S HER!!*' Sharon screamed.

'It's Wendy Carlisle!! that's the dress she was wearing when her body was found, this is unbelievable Max, you actually have footage of her leaving the bar with her killer!'

'Yes I do!' said Max, 'we now know that they definitely left the bar together at around 8.30 p m, we know our killer drives a black or grey sedan, I would say a 3 litre series but we will establish that for sure on Monday. He also dresses quite well, suit, shirt, tie, and if Charlotte Hoffman's description of him is anything to go by, he's also a bit of a Casanova who's approximately six foot four in height.'

'How can you tell that,' asked Sharon.? 'because of the angle of the camera, you don't have a full view of him, you can't see his face…'

'No, you can't…, which is why Mr Warring and I carried out a little experiment yesterday evening. I parked my car in the very same spot as the killer, and with Sam guiding me by phone, I took the exact same footsteps that our killer had taken as he and Wendy walked to the car.

Max took out the January 9th disc and inserted the one that they recorded yesterday.

'As you can see Sharon, the camera records me and the cut off point of recording shows my face up as far as my eye level, the difference in height between our killer and me being about five, perhaps six inches, agreed!!?'

'Yeah, go on,'

'Okay, so I'm five eleven and a bit yeah…, so that would make our killer roughly six foot four, six foot five tops.'

'But that still doesn't identify our killer, does it?'

'No it doesn't,' Max answered, 'but what it does do is…, it narrows down our killers profile significantly. This is huge Sharon, this is the breakthrough that we've been waiting for!'

'We're now looking for a tall, well to do, good looking guy, who dresses neatly and drives a dark coloured 2019 3 litre sedan.

Pete has already put out an APB to all checkpoints to concentrate their searches on dark coloured vehicles.

With this new information of the killer's profile, it now narrows down our search by about eighty per cent of the New York City male population at least, let's see you analyse that Professor Sanchez!!'

34

Natalie Johnson checked her watch for the umpteenth time, she was sitting on a park bench alongside her son Josh who only had eyes for the funfair carnival that was in full swing in the park across the road.

Josh had been her life since the day he first smiled at the world, the newness of his chubby rosy cheeks overshadowed only by the huge amount of hair that covered his head. It seemed that the only thing that he had inherited from his father was his soft brown skin and she was thankful for that.

Both Natalie and Josh had been looking forward to this for weeks. They had planned it about about a month ago, it was to form part of the bonding session between Josh and Danny, but Danny was running about fifteen minutes late and Natalie was getting a little worried because of his no-show. They had been together for about eight weeks now, and he was never late.

She had thought about ringing his mobile but decided against it, opting to wait a little longer. Maybe he was caught up in traffic, or perhaps something had come up at work, but the real cause of her anxiety was the fear that maybe Danny was having second thoughts about the bonding session, she was now starting to regret her suggestion that they would spend a day together, "like a family day out" as she recalls.

Natalie appreciated that Danny was a couple of years younger than her, plus the fact that Josh was a huge chunk of her life, maybe he had decided that he didn't need the baggage that came with their relationship.

Just as she was getting up to leave, her mobile rang, on the other end of the line was her Uncle Ross.

'Natalie, you need to get over to the County General straight away, it's Danny, he's been mugged, he's in a critical condition and the surgeons are taking him into theatre now, get here as fast as you can!!'

When Natalie eventually got to the emergency operating theatre and saw the surgeons and the NYPD gathering around room 101, she immediately knew that Danny was in serious trouble. She tried in vain to enter the room but was held back by her Uncle.

'Now is not a good time to go in and see him,' said Ross.

'He's been beaten pretty badly and has collapsed into a coma, the prognosis is not very good at the moment…'

'What happened?' asked Natalie, 'was it an attempted robbery? It can't have been just a random mugging in broad daylight?'

Ross sat his niece down on one of the plastic chairs that ran along the wall of the corridor, a nurse appeared and put two pills and a plastic cup of water into Natalie's hands.

'Please take these, they will help to calm you down, the Neurologist will be along in a few minutes to give you an up to date evaluation on Danny.'

'Who would do this Uncle Ross? Danny wouldn't harm a fly, what evil person would do such a thing?'

'Look, why don't we just stay calm,' Ross said, 'whoever did this to Danny will pay dearly sweetheart, I guarantee you, they will regret this, I'll make some enquiries, I have a few friends in the force, one being the assistant Commissioner, Sam Daly, I'll make a couple of calls later.'

Professor Nielson came through the doors and introduced himself to Natalie.

'At the moment, said the professor, 'Mr Montgomery is still in a coma, he has sustained very serious injuries to the upper part of the body, particularly his head, his skull is cracked and there is also haemorrhaging of the brain. At the moment, believe it or not, being in a coma is helping us to stem and control the bleeding. My team and I are going to operate on Danny in the next hour, the surgery will take between ten and twelve hours and only then will we be able to ascertain whether the operation will have been a success or not.

For now, there is not a lot either of you can do for Danny, so I would suggest you both get some rest because depending on the outcome, there could be a long road ahead!.

As the professor turned to walk towards the doors leading to the operating theatre, he felt a slight tap on his right shoulder and turned around to find himself face to face with Ross Kingsley.

'Can I help you Mr Kingsley?' the professor asked, a puzzled expression showing on his face.

Ross looked him straight in the eyes,

'Listen Doc, I want you to do your utmost to save the kid, I don't care what it takes, what it costs, money is no object, do you understand what I am saying Professor, money is not an object!'

Professor Nielson interrupted Ross,

'With respect sir, in this hospital we don't save people's lives for financial gain, we save people's lives because it's what we do, it's what we're good at!

'Now if you will excuse me, I need to go and scrub up!'

Ross watched as the surgeon walked through the automatic doors and disappear. He just stood there speechless, not sure how to react to this guy, the last person who took him with that type of threatening tone was his wife Rebecca, and she ended up in a chest freezer. But he slowly managed to break into a smile, he liked this guy's confident style, and as he walked back to the waiting room, he was happy in the knowledge that this Professor's no-nonsense attitude would be the main reason why Danny would survive this ordeal.

By the time Ross had got back to the waiting room, Natalie had escaped into a peaceful slumber, the couple of tablets she had taken earlier were now controlling her body. Ross opted to leave her on her own and walked back out into the corridor. As he walked past a row of grey coloured plastic chairs, he scrolled through the contact names on his mobile until Joey's name popped up and he pressed the dial button.

'Hello Joey, it's Ross Kingsley, I need you to do me a favour!'

Ross and Joey had worked together on and off over the years.

In his younger days, Joey was commonly known as "The Bruiser" a hired hand, who even though was a few bulbs short of a chandelier, was always guaranteed to get the job done. Nowadays he ran an almost legitimate security business, but not on the same magnitude as Ross, Joey's security operations included supplying body guards to V.I.P.'s, club doormen and in particular, debt collectors who would often used intimidating tactics to retrieve what was owed to his clients. Ross knew he could trust him.

'Hi Ross, what's happening?' asked Joey, in a hoarse voice, probably from the fact that he was a chain smoker and a cigarette never left his lips.

'I haven't heard from you in a while, how are you doing?'

'Listen Joey,' whispered Ross,

'I need a favour, I want you to handle something for me, something urgent!'

'Okay,' said Joey, 'I'm listening…'

'Earlier today in Queens, close to Rudi's coffee dock, a guy was beaten up pretty badly, I want you to find out who the mugger was?, I want the guy's name, and I want to know where he lives. I don't want you to have any contact with the guy, I don't want him ruffled up or anything, I just want his name and address, and Joey…, I would appreciate if you would handle this yourself. I want this to be between you and me, understood, and don't worry I will make it worth your while.'

'Yeah sure Ross, you know you can rely on me, I'll get cracking on it first thing in the morning…'

'No! no!! Joseph…, I don't think you understand, I want you to drop everything you are doing right now and get on it, this very minute, talk to your people, find out what the word on the street is and get back to me when you have the info, somebody in Queens knows exactly what went on earlier today and why. I'll be waiting for your call!'

Before Joey could get another word in, Ross had already hung up. He returned to the waiting room and sat down at the side of the makeshift bed.

He looked down on Natalie, stroking her cheek with the outside of his fingers, the soft complexion of her skin still managing to conceal the painful experiences that she had already endured in her young life, some which were because of him, stuff that he was ashamed of.

Again, old memories came flooding back, and not for the first time he began to compare Rebecca and Michelle, again dwelling on the fact that if he had married Michelle instead of that fucking drunken alcoholic, the girl he was now looking at could very well have been his daughter.

Although Ross blamed himself for some of her misfortunes, certain things had to be dealt with over the years, all for the greater good of the company. How was he to know that when he asked his IT manager to link everybody up to the one server, that the task would be assigned to Danny. If that task had been assigned to anybody else, it was probably a good bet that they would not be sitting in a hospital waiting room right now. As Ross sat there reminiscing, he reckoned it was going to be a long night, so decided to take a walk to the coffee dispenser down the corridor. After inserting the correct coinage, the white plastic cup dropped to the base and the coffee spewed out filling it to the top. Ross tasted the coffee and immediately realised that his money had been wasted, he threw the cup in the refuse bin and decided that he would take a walk outside the hospital, maybe pop into one of the bars along the street and try his luck there, hoping that the crushed coffee bean would resemble and taste like coffee as it should do.

He entered the first bar he came to on 42nd St and sat at the counter. The bar was quiet, not a whole lot of bums on seats, and if the truth be told, it had all the ambience of a funeral parlour. Over in one corner, two guys were busy playing pool, while in the opposite corner, an elderly couple were sipping on two half glasses of beer. Ross summoned the bartender and ordered his coffee.

There were two televisions, one at each end of the bar. The TV on the left was showing a baseball game, the one on the right was promoting some reality TV show where some wannabe celebrities were strutting around half naked, doing stuff that would surely embarrass their parents.

Ross opted for the baseball game which as it turned out, was not a bad game at all, come to think of it, neither was the coffee, it was definitely better than the piss water that they labelled as coffee back at the hospital. To sell that muck, he thought to himself, particularly at a hospital would surely have contravened five or six different laws contrary to food and drink legislation.

Ross watched the game until it was over, victory going to the Met's in a close game, he finished his coffee, dropped a ten dollar bill into the "war veteran's trust" glass jar and walked back to the hospital. When he arrived back, he headed straight to the waiting room. Natalie was still sleeping and hadn't moved an inch, it pleased him that she was still resting while the surgery was ongoing. He had imagined that on his return there was going to be some bad news about Danny, but he need not have worried.

Just as Ross had switched his phone back on silent, it started to buzz and he left the room.

'Christ Joey, that didn't take long! tell me that you have a name for me, please tell me you have the bastard's name!'

'It's a guy called Troy Denton, a bit of an asshole by all accounts, lives over in Queens, was overheard in a bar by one of my boy's, blabbing on about giving some young kid a hiding, apparently the kid was fucking his ex wife…, are you there Ross, can you hear me?'

'Yeah… I can hear you Joey, I can hear you loud and clear,' his body almost frozen by what Joey had just said.

'Thanks Joey,' said Ross, 'I'll be in touch,' and then hung up.

Ross walked up and down the hospital corridor, his head still spinning from what he had just been told. He finally decided to sit down on one of the grey plastic chairs in the hallway. For the next ten minutes he just sat there, staring at the cream coloured walls directly opposite, assessing the possible opportunity that had arisen, before eventually switching on his phone again and scrolling down through the contact names, He then pressed the dial button and slowly lifted the phone to his ear.

'Hey buddy, long time no hear, what can I do for you man…?'

asked the slurred voice on the other end of the line.

'Hello Troy..., I hear you've been a naughty little boy today, heard it on the grapevine that you had a bit of a run in with Danny Montgomery?'

'So what if I did!? the prick deserved everything he got, the little pussy didn't even put up a fight, I really enjoyed kicking his fucking little head in, why are you ringing Ross...? you want to try take me on as well, fancy your chances do you...? Just like Danny!'

'Hey, calm down Troy, on the contrary, in fact it's the opposite, I'm ringing you because I want to reward you, believe it or not you have done me a huge favour.'

'Reward me in what way?' asked the quickly sobering Troy,

'Well you're right, he is a pussy, and a fucking prick! The fucker was all over Natalie and little Josh, I could sense that he was forcing himself on her and I didn't trust him when he was alone with the kid, your kid, Troy...'

'Are you saying he's a Paedo?' asked Troy, 'are you telling me that...'

'Hang on a sec Troy,' interrupted Ross,

'I didn't exactly say that, but I have seen him hit the kid a couple of times, making the kid cry before locking him in his room.

Obviously that created a problem for me, until today that is, you my man have solved that problem and I believe you should be rewarded handsomely for it!'

'What kind of reward?' Troy asked, 'what kind of money are we talking about here?'

'Okay, listen carefully, I have a proposal for you..., because this is such a fucked up mess, Danny's in a coma, it's fifty fifty whether he's going to make it or not, the cops are all over the place asking questions, Natalie's in bits and Josh is been looked after by a nanny instead of being at home with his mother, the best thing you can do right now Troy, is up sticks, move out of New York altogether, maybe even as far as the west coast..'

'Hold on a second Ross, that's going to take a lot of money, I would have to be generously compensated if I were to even think about such a move, my home is here in New York. It's no secret that you're a wealthy man Ross, so let's talk figures, let's say a quarter of a million dollars…'

'How about let's talk about that tiny little fucking pea brain of yours instead shall we!?' snapped Ross. 'I don't need to clean up your fucking mess but I want to, for Natalie's sake, you do realise that if and when Danny regains consciousness and starts to talk, gives the cops a description of his attacker, it won't be long before they come looking for you Troy and you go to prison for a very long time, if I can find out who did this to Danny, then so can they. I hear prison is not the best place for a good looking boy like you Troy, a young fresh buck like you would have to be real careful not to drop the soap in the shower-room…'

Troy was silent, not saying anything, but he was certainly considering his options.

'Look, here's the deal' said Ross,

'I've got plenty of money in the safe at home, possibly as much as one hundred and twenty, maybe thirty thousand dollars, it's yours if you agree to leave New York, but it's gotta be tonight, you need to make a decision and you need to make it now!'

'You see, that's the difference between you and me Ross, I went on an all day bender today but I still know that I have about eighteen dollars in my pocket, whereas you on the other hand, treat money like confetti, you have so much money that you don't even know what's in your safe, it's plus or minus ten, maybe twenty grand and it doesn't even bother you!'

'That's just life Troy, and right now you're going to have to make a decision, a decision that decides how you live your life, how you fulfil your destiny. the clock is ticking Troy…, and you're running out of time.'

'Okay, okay let's do it!'

'Good, where are you now?'

'I'm in Neville's bar on 5th street.'

'Okay I'm just leaving the hospital, I'll see you outside the bar in fifteen minutes!'

Ross switched off his phone, took a quick peek in on Natalie to see that she was still sleeping and then walked to the hospital car park, got into his car and sat there for a couple of minutes, deep in thought.

Having carefully thought through what was going to happen in the next sixty minutes, optimising the time available, happily knowing that he had covered all the angles, Ross turned on the car's ignition, the pistons pumping the engine into life, powerfully slipping in and out of their cylinders as he drove off in the direction of 5th Avenue.

On the way, he looked at his watch, he estimated that all he needed was one hour, maybe less, and he would sort everything. As he approached Neville's bar, he could see Troy sitting on the window ledge.

'Get in Troy, we need to do this fast! Have you mentioned to anyone that you're leaving?'

'Just my flat mate, told him I was heading for the West Coast for a couple of months.'

'What about your belongings?' Ross asked.

'You're looking at them,' came the reply.

Troy was never a tidy dresser, his daily attire consisted of a royal blue denim shirt, an old pair of navy cord jeans and a pair of slipper shoes, all complimented by a silk multi-coloured bandanna which was wrapped around his black greasy head of hair. Take in the layer of crust that was evident on his upper lip, probably the result of some STD he picked up from a hooker, he looked like shit.

'Mind if I smoke Ross?' Troy asked, rolling a reefer with his nicotine stained fingers before lighting up with one of those cheap fuel lighters.

Although he despised the smell of cigarette smoke, Ross decided to ignore the request, the scumbag had lit up anyway, and punishing him for that would be something that he would enjoy later.

By the time they arrived at the gates of the house, Troy was asleep. Although their marriage was a short one, Natalie had never mentioned that Troy would grind his teeth together when he was asleep, maybe it was his way of getting rid of some of the plaque that was already embedded in his rotting teeth. It was just another irritating habit that Ross was so looking forward to rectifying once they got to the house.

Ross looked across at him, thinking, 'what a fucking nasty little prick, what did Natalie ever see in this piece of garbage, not a single grey cell in his head, had never contributed anything to society, not even to his own kid.

Ross shook him a little to wake him up.

It was enough to startle Troy, who was now rubbing his eyes with his hands before realising where he was.

'I didn't know you had kept this house Ross, didn't you and that sexy brunette get married and move across the city?'

Ross didn't answer.

As the car careered up the driveway, Troy let the window down and stuck his head out, inhaling the night air,

'Gee Ross, smelling those roses is like smelling the dough!! I always loved coming to this house, it always made me feel good, coming here with Natalie was like paying a visit to the local ATM, the money just spat itself out!'

Those couple of words reminded Ross just how much of a bloodsucking leech Troy really was, vermin like him were a scourge on society and needed to be eradicated, taken out of circulation. Those thoughts alone convinced Ross that his next course of action would without doubt be the correct one.

They entered the house and headed for the drawing room, the interior lighting system coming on automatically.

'Wow'!! Blabbered Troy out loud, 'I had forgotten what this place was like, no shortage of money spared on this place!'

'C'mon, let's get this over with, said Ross as he walked over to the far side of the room, opened the framed tinted glass windows of a cabinet that revealed a small combination safe.

Troy, as expected, headed straight for the drinks cabinet, where he could see lines of bottles standing in rows. Picking up various brands at random, Troy scrutinised the label on each bottle, before settling on an old favourite.

'Mind if I pour myself a bourbon, Ross?' asked Troy, in a tone that suggested that he was having one anyway, regardless of the answer.

'Yeah, help yourself and pour me one while you're at it, it's been one hell of a day.'

'Got any ice?' asked Troy, 'the ice bucket is empty!'

'Yeah I'll just go get some from the freezer, won't be a sec.'

While getting the ice from the freezer in the kitchen, Ross was watching Troy on camera, watching him sprint over to the safe and stuffing two wads of hundred dollar bills into his pockets, Ross smiled as he carefully selected the ice cubes that were stored in their own little compartment in the freezer.

When he arrived back in the drawing room, Troy was sitting on the couch and Ross placed the bucket of ice cubes on the table.

Using his dirty bloodied fingers, Troy chucked some ice cubes into his bourbon and swallowed it down in one go.

'Mind if I have another, I'm kinda thirsty,' Troy asked in a flippant manner of respect..

'Go ahead, help yourself,' answered Ross, watching Troy's every move.

This time Troy walked around the table passing the safe, 'You got a nice bit of jewellery and stuff stashed in there as well.'

'Yes, belonged to my late wife, Rebecca. It's of sentimental value, I would never part with any of it.'

Troy brought the bottle of bourbon to the table, sat himself down and poured himself another generous glass of alcohol.

Ross took his glass and sipped some bourbon,

'Aren't you having any ice Ross? didn't you always drink your bourbon with ice.?'

'Yeah, normally I would, but I've got this sensitive tooth and anything cold drives it crazy. Got a dental appointment first thing in the morning, you certainly like your ice Troy,'

'Yeah bourbon on its own is okay but the ice gives it that something, that special kick that it deserves,'

'Couldn't agree more Troy, couldn't agree more!'

As Ross walked towards the cabinet, he was looking at the mirror close by, keeping an eye on Troy as he mixed his drinks, popping in three or four ice cubes at a time and gulping down the contents before repeating the exercise.

Troy sat on the couch as he watched Ross take wads of one hundred dollar bills from the safe and place them on the table. Happy images went flashing through his brain as to how he was going to spend all this lovely dough on the West Coast, Casinos, bars, beaches and of course, all those beautiful women.

Still sipping on his bourbon, Troy watched gleefully as Ross counted out one hundred and eighty thousand dollars, made up in wads of twenty thousand and held neatly together by various coloured rubber bands. Ross pushed the wads across the table towards Troy, who was licking his scabby lips, savouring the moment, he had never seen that amount of money in his life. He picked up one of the wads, flicked through it with his thumb before landing a prolonged smacker of a kiss on the face of Benjamin Franklin.

While Ross walked back across the room to close the safe, Troy noticed the baseball bat nestling against the ruby flowered cushion pouf, close to the far end of the table, he knew there was plenty more money to be had, could be up to half a million bucks in that safe including the gold items and the jewellery, all he had to do was to get rid of Ross, one swift movement across the room and smack..., Ross's head would explode wide open, a second blow would surely kill him off!

If he was going to do it, it would have to be now but he couldn't, as much as he wanted to, he couldn't. No matter how hard his brain urged his legs to get up, his body muscles did not obey its commands. Ross closed the safe and turned to face Troy,

'You thought about it didn't you? you thought about it, you little fuck!! You wanted to smash that bat right into the back of my skull, finish me off and run with the contents of the safe, I watched you in the mirror, I could see it in your eyes, you wanted to, but you can't, can you Troy?'

'You're fucked, Troy! The bat that you found so tempting, it belongs to me and that fucked up head of yours is my baseball. Thanks to you it looks like it's going to be another home run for me tonight!'

'But… but hang on… I thought you and me had a deal, you told me that you were happy that I did a such good job on the Irishman, that it got you and Natalie off the hook, we had a deal Ross, you can't renege on it now… why the fuck can't I move my arms and legs!!?'

'Don't worry Troy, you won't be like this for long.'

'You mean it's gonna wear off? I'll be able to move my arms and legs again…?' asked Troy, his words slowly becoming incoherent, the blood fully drained from his ashen face, a face that was now showing a sense of fear and anxiety.

In just a couple of minutes, his reversal of fortune had turned one hundred and eighty degrees and he was now at the mercy of his captor.

He made one more attempt to stand up, but it was a feeble one, he wasn't moving anywhere.

'Well that's not exactly what I meant,' answered Ross, as he slowly bent over and picked up the aluminium baseball bat, flexing his muscles as he did so.

'There is an antitoxin that you can use, but you wont be needing it, not today, today is your day of atonement. You see Troy, in lots of ways, you and I are alike, we both possess this ugly streak that's embedded in our DNA, we both possess that tendency to want to destroy human life but…, that's where our similarities end. Unlike me, you lack a moral compass, you maim and kill people without reason or remorse, you don't care whether they have lived a good life or not, for you death has no boundaries, no limits, no breaking points, whereas when I carry out a violent act, it is for a reason, it has a purpose, it has motive. The people I have killed have died for a reason, they too had a nasty streak hibernating inside them, be it greed, avarice, selfishness, they all had the ability to harm people and not care about the implications of their actions.

Those perpetrators had to pay for their crimes and so will you, when you married Natalie you made her life hell, remember when she was pregnant with Josh, you beat her so badly, her unborn baby nearly died, now it's your turn Troy, it's your turn to experience that evil streak that we both possess, it's time to experience the pain, the horror, the realisation that you are going to die!

Troy looked up at Ross and started to cry, he was trying very hard to distinguish between what was fact and what was fiction, desperately hoping that he was on one of those bad acid trips that fucked him over the cliff every now and again, maybe he had bought some cheap shit that had been passed off as good gear while his dilated pupils were pleading to his captor, begging him to let him live. Ross just smiled, that compulsive rage was now racing through his body, like a bolt of lightning shooting across the sky. Ross raised his hands above his head and let rip, the blunt force of the aluminium baseball bat connecting with Troy's jawline sent at least six of his bottom teeth shooting across the room in all directions. Even before his brain had received the signal to experience the pain of such brute force, the second blow had cracked his skull wide open while the compelling and clinical execution of the third and fourth blows blew him right off the couch and onto the floor. The final blow, the "coup de grace", the punishment for smoking in his car, connected with the back of the exploding cranium, completing the job.

Troy's body stretched limply out on the ground, blood spatters along with fragments of flesh and bone slid down the sticky velvet back supports of the couch, Ross could smell the odour of the fresh blood as his nostrils soaked up the contaminated air in the room.

That adrenalin of death was once again pumping through his entire body, ebbing and flowing through his veins as he surveyed the bloodied remains of his latest fix, Ross leaned over his prey, a victim of his own evil making, he wanted, he craved so much to howl at the top of his voice, like a werewolf would howl at a full moon, but he somehow managed to compose himself, bringing his breathing pattern back to normality.

Using a wet towel, he wiped the blood spatters and the fragments of skull bone from the aluminium bat, marvelling on how such a lightweight piece of metal could inflict such horrific injuries on a person's body.

It even crossed his mind that if he had not taken the technology path as his mantle in life, he would have been a phenomenal baseball player and there was no doubt he thought, that if Troy was still alive, he would certainly have agreed. It hadn't taken long to wrap the body in the heavy duty plastic sheeting and he bound it together with a roll of grey plumber's tape. Picking the body up and slinging it over his shoulder, he proceeded to carry the corpse downstairs to the basement, bringing back the memories of how he had carried Rebecca to her resting place all those years ago.

When he got to the basement, he lifted the freezer lid and dumped Troy's body in on top of Rebeccas.

'Rebecca, say hello to Troy, Troy say hello to Rebecca. Hope you two can manage to get on together and keep each other warm.'

Ross had a good giggle at that, closed the lid down and went back upstairs.

After he had showered and dressed himself in similar attire to what he had worn earlier, a dark suit, white shirt, black tie and black shoes, it would be a very observing eye, he thought, that would detect his change of clothes in the last couple of hours. It was around eight thirty pm when Ross arrived back at the hospital. He parked his car in the same spot where it was parked earlier, and walked briskly back through the front doors of the hospital.

The fact that nobody, particularly Natalie had tried to contact him while he was absent, meant there was at the very least no change in Danny's condition and in all probability, Natalie was still sleeping.

Sure enough, when he re-entered the room, it looked like Natalie hadn't stirred in her sleep at all. Ross took the time to look into the cracked mirror which hung on the wall above the wash basin, he brushed back his hair and straightened his tie. The collar of his shirt rubbing against the stubble protruding from his neck and chin as he did so, while the waves of adrenalin continued to flow sweetly through his veins. As he looked deep into the mirror, the man looking back at him began to smile, showing no signs of compunction whatsoever.

What he had done tonight would go some way in compensating Natalie for what had happened in her life all those years ago, but what also pleased him, without getting complacent, was that he now felt invincible, untouchable, undetectable, he was so far ahead of the cops, so far ahead of the law that he could continue this for years.

However, he decided not to complicate matters, for now he would curtail his moods, stay focused on his original plan and bring it to a close. He would live on the straight and narrow for awhile, take a nice holiday, then come back refreshed, perhaps volunteer to do some community work for the good people of New York City. Still looking in the mirror, he even contemplated selling the company to a consortium or a conglomerate, this would free up his time to take up new hobbies, hobbies that would compliment his growing array of skills.

At four thirty am, Professor Nielsen appeared through the automatic doors and walked towards the waiting room. Ross saw him coming and woke Natalie out of her slumber.

Even before the professor had said a word, Ross knew by his demeanour that the operation had gone well. The professor informed them that there were no complications during the surgery, and that everything had gone according to plan.

'Has the bleeding stopped?' asked Natalie.

'Yes, we did manage to stem the bleeding although initially, he had lost a lot of blood before we got him to theatre. Whether that has gone against him, I'm afraid it's too early to call, all I can say at the moment is that Danny is out of the coma, he is stable and sleeping on his own terms. We will obviously continue to monitor his condition and he is in very good hands.'

Natalie hugged and thanked Professor Nielson before deciding that she would stay the night, she wanted to be there for Danny when he opened his eyes.

With his Shangri- la securely locked up and fully alarmed, Ross decided that he too would stay the night, he would sort the bodies later. He now realised that after all those years spent in cold storage, Rebecca's body, along with Troy's would have to be moved, taken far away from the house and buried so deep that the two bodies would never be found, maybe he would take them both out on the boat and drop them fully laden in chains, to the bottom of the Hudson River.

This whole messy business with Danny and Troy was not welcome or helpful to his plans, deep inside he knew he had acted on impulse, he had stepped outside his comfort zone and his actions tonight were ill-judged and reckless in the greater scheme of things. He was disappointed that he had lacked the discipline required, however, he saw it only as a minor distraction and remained happy in the knowledge that although Troy's killing was not planned or executed like the others, he could still experience the buzz of the kill.

35

April

It was just after 9.30am when Max arrived at the city morgue, heading straight for Theatre 1. Sharon had arrived minutes earlier and had already scrubbed up, the blood stained scalpel in her right hand indicating to him that she had already began the autopsy. As usual, she was dressed in her white cotton suit with the legs tucked neatly into her green rubber boots. It was in this very room that they had met for the first time almost ten years ago when they first realised that they had at least one thing in common.

That day, on the same cold grey slab, lay a female corpse, the body of a young woman who had been repeatedly gang-raped before been brutally kicked to death as she walked home the night before. Her name was Jessica Barnes, she was nineteen years old and had been out celebrating with her college friends.

Sharon and Max had made a pact that day. They both agreed they would not rest until they had brought this young woman's killers to justice. In just under three months after Jessica's death, her killers appeared in court, three youths from Queens, who had been apprehended and arrested by Max and charged with her murder.

The case ran for about six weeks, the evidence gathered by Max, backed up by the unchallenged forensic evidence presented by Sharon, guaranteed that there would be only one verdict returned.

The jury of eight men and four women, returned a unanimous verdict of guilty and the young men were sentenced to three life sentences each for their vile and evil acts. In other words, they would never see the outside of a prison again. That verdict was the start of a very successful partnership of criminal investigations and closures for Sharon and Max, they had a ninety eight per cent success rate regarding convictions, the highest in the country, it would also mark the beginning of their relationship and it had left Max pondering what a pity that their short fiery relationship didn't blossom as much as their crime detection efforts had.

Unlike Max, the passage of time had been more than generous to Sharon, her career had flourished and she was widely acknowledged as one of the top pathologists in the country, while retaining her youthful good looks…, especially when she wore those green rubber boots in the morgue. There was something about watching her work while wearing those boots that turned him on, and they were probably the one thing that attracted him to her in the first place. Maybe it was the fluorescent lighting in the mortuary that made her graceful manner all the more appealing. Whatever it was, she had it in abundance.

She once ironically described the mortuary as her "Oasis of life", it was the one place in the world where she could find peace and tranquillity, where she could open her heart to those that were laid out on the slabs or in the refrigerated coffins that surrounded her, how they would quietly listen as she confided in them, sharing everything about her own life, her hopes, her fears, knowing her secrets were safe. In return for listening to her silent voice, her patients would be happy knowing that the pathologist would give them a flawless post-mortem examination that would help catch their killer and allow them, the victims, to begin their journey to the other side.

'Good morning Max,' said Sharon, 'you got my message then?' her grim face only telling half the story.

'Well not exactly,' Max answered, 'it was Pete who you can thank for that, his call woke me just as I had finally managed to fall asleep.'

'So how did you know I was here if you didn't get my message..?' Sharon asked, looking a little bit confused.

'Pete told me, he said the SS team had been and gone and I should head straight here…,' Max shut his mouth immediately, having just realised what he had said, a momentary lapse of concentration while he checked his pager and he had spilled the beans.

'What do you mean, the SS team…?' Sharon asked, lifting her

eyebrows, the pupils in her eyes expanding as she stared in the direction of the detective.

'Is that what you guy's call us downtown, you compare us to a bunch of Nazi criminals!!?' asked Sharon, shaking her head slowly from side to side.

'No no,' Max blurted out, trying to conceal his annoyance at what he had said, while realising he had just stepped into a shit storm.

'The SS reference is for your initials, Sharon Stillman, I'm not sure if you remember this Sharon, but a couple of years back, you berated a young rookie officer for not closing off a crime scene sooner than he did and vital evidence was contaminated, the rollicking you gave him that day scared the shit out of him so much, that the next time you arrived at a scene, the young officer who also happened to be there whispered out loud, 'watch it fella's, the SS team have arrived, and it's stuck ever since.'

The reaction on Sharon's face assured Max that he could relax, she saw the funny side of the story and continued to make an incision across the murdered victim's chest.

'What have we got here?' Max asked.

'It's our fourth victim,' Sharon answered, 'found close to Tomkins Cove, discovered by an early morning jogger.

'Any chance it's a copy killing?'

'Absolutely not, has all the traits of our Ghost, no deviation whatsoever from his M.O.'

'What about her digestive system, did she by chance have something to eat?'

'No nothing, just plenty of alcohol consumed, just like the others.'

Sharon pointed to the plastic pouch on the table, opposite the grey slab.

'You might want to look at that!'

Max walked over to the table, picked up the pouch and held it up just above eye level. It was what he had already knew, as he studied the contents of the card, it was as if the Ram was looking straight back and laughing at him. Max looked down on the woman's body spread out on the slab. Sharon was right he thought, definitely the same M.O. as the other girls, even though her face was beaten to a pulp, you could tell she was pretty, just like the others. Max always questioned whether dead people went into hibernation when they died, maybe go to sleep for awhile, as in a state of limbo before they set out on their final journey. For now, he couldn't answer that question, but knew that some day like everybody else, he would find the answer.

Max bent his knees, putting his mouth close to the victim's ear, and he whispered softly,

'Hello Miss Aries, guess what? Not only are you on the local news today, but you've also made the headline news on all the big networks this morning, I'm so sorry that I couldn't save you, I'm sorry that I haven't found your killer yet, but I promise you I will, I'm going to catch the bastard soon, real soon, and when I do, I promise you, and the other girls, that he will pay dearly for his crimes.

'I see our killer has left his little verse for us again, outlining the specific trait's of the Ram, "Courage," "Forceful," "Passionate" and "Reckless", Max quietly asked himself which of those qualities had got her killed?, Was it her passion, her recklessness maybe, or was it a combination of them all?

'Her name is Shirley Lentz, lives over in Queens…'

'You mean lived over in Queens!' Max corrected her,

'Whichever' Sharon answered, 'she was a college lecturer in marketing finance, which again tells us that "Silas" likes his women to be well qualified in their profession, all four were college educated, successful in their jobs and highly respected by their work colleagues.'

'Married?'

'No, single, just like the others.'

'Bit of a coincidence maybe, all our girls being single.'

'Maybe,' Sharon answered.

'But more than likely it's not,' said Max, 'it's easier to strike up a conversation with a single person than someone that's married or in a relationship, the question is, where is he selecting them from? Which brings us back to the singles clubs, the dating agencies which we have already checked out without success.

'Charlotte Hoffman told her mother that she had met this new guy a couple of days earlier, but she never told her how or where.'

'I'm assuming the post mortem report will be the same as the others, unless Ms Aries has somehow left us a clue...' asked Max.

'I wish I could give you something to go on Max, but with the exception of Wendy Carlisle, judging by her head injuries, I'm guessing cause of death is the same as the previous two victims, incapacitated to some degree, followed by severe blows to the head, possibly with the same weapon, then the killer kneels over them and finishes them off by suffocating them, he wants his victims to look at him as they gasp for air while he squeezes the last bit of life out of them with his bare hands.'

'DNA?' asked Max, knowing he was clutching at straws.

'Haven't got that far yet, but with what I'm looking at right now, I would say no, absolutely nothing!'

Max rested on the far corner of the slab, feeling totally deflated, almost lethargic.

'We're now in April, the fourth month of the year and we have four dead women, who, with the exception of the first victim, showed no signs of putting up a struggle, showed no resistance whatsoever.

They just seemed to have accepted their fate, conceded defeat to the killer, whilst Wendy Carlisle on the other hand, was bound, not once, but twice, yet fought with everything she had to stay alive, apart from that there was no difference between her and the other three women.? the question is..., why, after killing Wendy, did he change his M.O. for his next three victims?'

'Maybe he didn't!' said Sharon.

Our first victim dies of asphyxiation, even though, unlike the others, she puts up one hell of a struggle, the killer doesn't use another weapon, only his hands, it's as if he went berserk, something happened that made him lose control, she wasn't meant to die that way, we know that she was bound twice, what if, when she escaped, she forced him to kill her that way, maybe she didn't want to give her killer the opportunity, the option of killing her the way he had planned.'

'We're missing something here Sharon,' said Max as he stepped away from the slab and paced up and down the theatre, we need to go back to the beginning, start again!

Sharon looked at Max, on any other day he would be bragging about how many notchs he had on his belt, how many criminals he had put behind bars, she knew him so well, she could see the frustration of what he was going through, she had seen him get uptight about different situations in the past, but this was different, his incisiveness was missing, there was an edginess to his character she had never seen before, and she knew these murders were biting deep into his soul, piercing his very heart, like a dagger. Max was one of those guys who took his work home, made everything personal, particularly when it came to murder investigations, and she had no doubt that even now, he would hold himself responsible, laden himself with guilt and possibly take some of the blame for the girls deaths. Sharon sensed that during the last couple of weeks, Max had lost some of his flair, his desire, the dynamics of his investigative skills were not apparent this time round, and she worried about him.

'Can I ask you a straight question Max' she asked.

'Go ahead,'

'If you were in a room, standing face to face with our serial killer, with Silas, just the two of you, no cameras, no audio tapes, no witnesses, and you were one hundred percent sure that he was guilty, what would be your preferred option of punishment for his crimes.?'

'Punishment..., in what way?'

'It's a simple question Max, would you bring him in alive and cuffed or would you bring him in wrapped in a body bag?'

Max did not commit himself to an answer, he just stood there, arms folded, looking downwards.

'How are you coping, Max?'

'Why do you ask?' he said, looking up at her with a condescending stare.

'When was the last time you took a holiday, Max?' 'You look tired, maybe you should think about taking a break for a few days, your body needs to rest, you need to clear your head!'

Max's stare had got darker and deeper.

'Hey don't look at me like that!' snapped Sharon.

'Look.., all I'm saying is, let someone else take the flak, if only for a few days, take a back seat for awhile and when you come back, things may not look so bleak.

'Just remember, you've joined an elite group of people, not every cop gets the opportunity to be the leading investigator in the hunt for a serial killer!'

'This guy is up there with the best of them, killers like John Wayne Gacey, Ted Bundy, Jeffrey Dahmer,

Those sons of bitches are few and far between, they are in a different league to your average weekend drunken brawl killer, they have one goal in life, they come along once in a generation, seeking recognition, seeking salvation, some are not highly educated, some come from poor family backgrounds while others are sexually abused and some, well, they just try and pin the blame on adolescent, but this guy is none of that!

He's smart, he's educated, he's a man of affluence, a man of means, and we know he drives around in a fancy car.'

'Now if the killings continue, and there is no reason for them not to, unless of course we get a lucky break and catch the motherfucker in the meantime, his next victim is going to be a Taurus correct...? so we have roughly two and a half weeks to apprehend him.'

'That's all very fine' Max said, 'but even though the majority of the public can relate to Gacey, Bundy or Damhler, I bet nobody can remember the people that caught them.'

'That's exactly my point Max, when we catch this son of a bitch, everybody will remember Max Hammond, everybody will know who brought those women's killer to justice, but that's not going to happen if the lead investigator is physically and mentally fucked...!! so what I'm simply saying is this, it's Sunday, go home!! if you want to flush this fucker out into the open, you need to be at your best, so my advice is, take a couple of days off, go home Max..., get some rest and give me a call on Wednesday!'

36

May

Shelley Davidson didn't look anything like a Taurus. Max could tell that the brunette had been a timid, almost petite individual, who probably wouldn't hurt a fly, nothing to suggest that she had a bullish disposition. Although her facial injuries were severe, he could tell that she had put in the effort to impress her killer. It was evident that she had spent plenty of time applying make-up before she met him. Shelley wore a reddish burgundy dress that stopped just above the knees, her red coloured, high heel shoes complimenting her dress to perfection. Although all the victims were placed in similar positions on the ground, this one was different, Shelley's body had been laid out in a much more dignified fashion, almost tastefully, by her killer, her arms and hands folded, resting neatly on her chest, her legs joined together. For a killer to carry his victim to a burial site, even in darkness was plucky, but to take the time to arrange the body in that position showed all the traits of a psychopath. Again the killer did not disappoint with his Zodiac message. It was a bright red card, showing an angry bull bellowing through its nose, a shiny silver metal ring pierced through the bull's septum. Max rang Professor Sanchez immediately, telling her about the positioning of the body.

'What do you think Professor, why would he change now? It can't be out of respect surely, how can you respect somebody and end up killing them?'

'It's got nothing to do with the victim that you are looking at' said the professor, 'but it may have something to do with his next target, his Gemini, it's possible that he knows her and when he kills her, he will lay her out with dignity. What you are looking at, is the trial run, he's preparing for his final victim, he knows that it's coming to an end, his evil crusade is almost over, his jigsaw is almost complete! Detective, if you don't catch him by the end of the Gemini phase and he achieves his goal, then there is a very good chance that you will lose him forever!'

37

June

'Happy Birthday sweetheart,' whispered Eve, as she kissed Ross on the cheek.

'How does it feel to be a quinquagenarian today? I've got a nice surprise lined up for you tonight.'

'Like what?'

'Oh, you'll just have to wait and see, won't you my darling, but I guarantee that you will not be disappointed' answered Eve.

Ross rested his hands on Eve's hips and kissed her on the lips,

'And I've got a nice surprise for you as well, and just like me, you too will also have to wait.'

'Oh, my darling Ross, you do spoil me don't you…, said Eve as she picked up her purse and keys from the table.

'Where are you going now?

'I'm going to the shopping mall to buy a new dress for tonight, if I go now I should be back around four.'

Excellent' Ross said, 'that should give me enough time to prepare as well.'

Ross watched Eve on camera as she drove out of the underground car park and headed downtown.

He then asked himself the question, is she really going downtown to buy a dress or is she meeting loverboy for a quick fuck, given that her birthday was in a couple of days, maybe Cliff wanted to give her an early birthday fuck!! He would find out soon enough!

However, that didn't matter now as he took the small plastic tube from his pocket and mixed the solution of nerve toxin with a measured amount of water, poured the liquid into an ice cube tray and put it in the freezer. It was time for the last piece of the jigsaw, he had chosen his birthday to carry out his final act of retribution.

As he had expected, Eve returned empty handed a couple of hours later, the rosy flushness on her face telling him what he already knew. There was no dress to be bought, there never was, his wife had just spent the last couple of hours fucking loverboy, but he didn't mind, it reminded him of why he had started this in the first place. The final scene was playing out nicely, in a couple of hours, Eve Kingsley would be found brutally murdered, just like the others, leaving Ross a widower for the second time, another victim of our evil society, and the good people of New York would mourn and share in his grief.

Ross had decided that he would be patient with Cliff, he couldn't take the chance that nobody else knew about the affair. He figured that when women have affairs, they will always confide in at least one of their female friends. They look to them for advice, for support, they need to hear the friend tell them they are doing the right thing, while men on the other hand, just want to brag to all their buddies, boasting about how good a shag their young mistress is.

To kill 'loverboy' now could pose problems. Ross didn't want the cops sniffing around so he was prepared to wait a year, perhaps even two before exacting revenge on the slimeball.

'Sweetheart', shouted Eve from the bedroom, 'I'm dying for a gin and tonic, will you pour me one.?'

Ross smiled, the irony of it, 'dying for a gin and tonic,' in a couple of minutes she would be dying from a gin and tonic. He poured a healthy measure of gin into a glass and added some tonic, he then walked to the fridge, where he pulled the ice cube tray from the freezer cabinet.

'Perfect,' he whispered to himself as he dropped four ice cubes into the glass.

When Eve returned to the living room a couple of minutes later, Ross was sitting down reading a car magazine, sipping on his favourite "Old Fashioned" bourbon, he didn't even look up to acknowledge her presence.

Eve sat in the chair opposite, lifting her gin and tonic to her mouth, taking a large swig from the glass. Although Ross had his head stuck in the magazine, he was looking out of the corner of his eye, his heart pounding as his wife put the glass to her lips for a second time, taking another large swig, that should do it he thought, there was no turning back now, give it another couple of minutes and she won't be able to move.

'Since when have you taken up baseball?' laughed Eve, pointing in the direction of the baseball bat that lay on the ground behind Ross's chair.

'Oh, I've been practising with it for a couple of months now,' Ross answered, slowly picking the bat up and tapping it on his knee, 'in fact I'm getting quite good at it, especially the accuracy of my swing which is improving all the time, why don't you finish that drink and I'll pour you another!'

'But, you don't have the balls for it, do you Ross?'

'What do you mean by that!!?,' Ross asked, his blood slowly starting to rise.

'Well, you don't have any balls, just the bat, how can you improve your swing if you don't have the balls in the first place!!?'

Ross sensed that she was now riling him, taking the piss, just like Rebecca, goading him on, making fun of the fact that she had just been with Cliff, her lover, who had just fucked her brains out in the middle of the afternoon, and on his birthday, of all days!

Ross could now feel the emotional rage that was beginning to simmer inside him, his heart was pounding relentlessly, the warm fast flowing blood was racing through his veins.

Eve finished her drink and went to pass the glass to Ross, but it fell from her hand and onto the carpet. 'Wow!' Eve said, 'that drink has certainly gone to my head, I don't know what's coming over me.'

Ross picked up the baseball bat, walked to the other side of the table and pushed the bat into Eve's chest, forcing her back into the chair.

It was then she realised she was unable to move, she couldn't recover her position, she was powerless but still possessed her thought and speech faculties.

'What's happening to me? Why can't I move? why can't I get up? She asked, now frightened and scared as she looked at her husband who was now smiling into her face. It wasn't so much the hideous smile that freaked her, but the cold evil empty stare that was looking into her eyes, she had never witnessed that before.

'Where were you today Eve?' Ross asked, turning the batting end of the baseball bat slowly in the palm of his left hand, the velvet cloth polishing a nice shine that gleamed all the way down the shank before he placed the bat gently on the table.

'I went shopping, you know that, I told you earlier! I went to Jefferson's shopping mall, I tried on some dresses, fitted on some shoes, but didn't find anything that I liked.

'Why can't I move...?'

Ross slowly picked up the baseball bat, tapping the batting end against her forehead a couple of times, he then knelt in front of her and took off her shoes,

'What size shoe are you Eve?'

'I'm a four, you know that, why are you asking?'

'Because..., If you keep lying to me you're going to be needing at least a size eight,' answered Ross as the baseball bat came crashing down on her left foot with tremendous force, breaking at least three of her toes. Although the toxin had sent Eve into a state of paralysis, it did not numb the senses and the excruciating pain raced relentlessly through her body. Eve screamed at the highest pitch that her voice box would allow, but it would all be in vain.

Some months earlier, Ross had got the apartment soundproofed, so nobody was going to hear her cries for help. He picked up the TV remote and pointed it in the direction of the television, he pressed the little green button and the huge colourful screen came alive.

Ross deliberately crouched down on his knees next to Eve, he was so close to her that she could smell the 'Old Fashioned' cocktail on his breath.

'Let's watch some TV shall we?'

They both watched the recording from the overhead drone that had followed her car for a couple of miles before pulling into a car park. The drone's camera zoomed in on her as she got out of her car and walked across to the green coloured Sedan, looking around before she got in.

'Cliff has a green sedan, hasn't he?' asked Ross as they watched the car drive off until it reached "The Rendezvous" motel on Jefferson Drive.

'*Turn it off!!*' shouted Eve, 'turn the fucking thing off' as the tears streamed down her face.

'Aren't drones a wonderful invention' said Ross, as he tightly clenched hundreds of strands of her long dark hair, jerking her head backwards against the base of the couch.

'However the downside is, they're going to put a lot of Private Dicks out of business!'

'Nowadays, everybody can watch what everybody else is up to, and they don't even have to leave the house, and as we can see, lover boy wasn't very good at keeping his dick private, was he!!?'

'How did you know? how the fuck did you figure it out?' asked Eve.

'Oh it was easy, I had it figured just before last Christmas, remember when I came home unexpectedly and walked in on yourself and Clifford? I had flown back earlier than planned from L.A. and walked in on both of you, you and loverboy were just about to tear each other's clothes off when I interrupted your lustful afternoon.

In fairness Eve, I gotta hand it to you, how quickly you were able to make up that interior decorating shit, while Cliff just nodded his head in agreement to everything you said. Actually, it was Cliff who gave the game away, it was Cliff who spilled the beans.'

'But how? He never said anything to me, he never even mentioned that he had spoken to you since that day.'

'Well that's true in a sense, but he did something that day while he was in the apartment with you. Do you remember when I walked in that afternoon and Cliff had to go to the bathroom before he left.?'

'Yes, I think so' answered Eve, 'why is that significant?'

'When he returned from the bathroom, I asked him if he had done any work in the other apartments and his reply was an emphatic NO! in fact, he said it was his first time ever being in the neighbourhood.'

'So what? what are you getting at?' asked Eve.

'When I arrived home that day, you said that you had both arrived just a couple of minutes earlier than me, that's what you wanted me to believe, but we now know that's not true, and I will tell you why.

If both of you had arrived home just minutes earlier, and it was loverboy's first time in the neighbourhood, how the fuck did he know how to get to the bathroom when neither you or I gave him directions as to where it was!

He went straight to the bathroom, without giving it a thought, isn't that extraordinary Eve...? you could have put a blindfold over his eyes and he would still have made his way to the bathroom, he knew exactly where it was!

So you tell me Eve, you tell me exactly what was significant about that, come on Eve spit it out, no use denying it now, the fucking game is up!'

'It meant it wasn't the first time he had been in the apartment' stuttered Eve.

'Correct, and from that day, Eve, the day lover boy decided to go for a piss, I had made my mind up that you were going to die!'

'How many times was he here Eve, how many times did you fuck him in our bed!!?'

'Does it really matter now?'

'Yes, it does matter, it matters to me..., do you know, that one of the last things Rebecca said to me before I killed her..., she said you were a filthy fucking whore and she was right, she may not have got many things right in her life, Eve, but she certainly hit the nail on the head when she was describing you!'

38

'What do you mean when you say, *"before I killed her"*? everybody knows that Rebecca died along with her sister when the South Tower was hit on 9/11, everybody knows that! Rebecca's DNA was positively identified, you have the Coroner's letter to prove that, don't you remember? Weren't you the hero of the hour, camera coverage of your heroic rescue efforts witnessed across the world. I don't believe you, you're just trying to scare me.

Ross stooped down slowly towards Eve and whispered in her ear,

'The DNA match that they found in the debris of the South Tower belonged to her sister Michelle, not Rebecca, but, because they were twins born from the same egg, it meant that they both shared the same DNA, Rebecca was dead hours before the Towers were hit. I drowned her in the bathtub in the early morning hours of Tuesday, 9/11. When the terrorists flew the planes into the buildings, I saw the perfect opportunity opening up in front of me, I created the perfect alibi, that Tuesday morning the world acknowledged me as a great American hero, watching in awe, as I pulled people from the water, ferrying them to safety.'

'But why Ross?, why did you have to kill her?'

'I did it for you Eve, I killed her for you! for *us*!'

'Why didn't you just divorce her, that's what normal people do.? but you're not normal..., are you Ross?'

'You just don't understand Eve, do you? It was because of you, she was divorcing me because she found out about you, she found out about us! Rebecca had already started divorce proceedings against me the day before 9/11, I would have lost control of the Company, I would have lost everything, her father would probably have sent me to work in the mail room and I was not going to allow that to happen.'

'But what did you do with her body? how did you get rid of it?

did you bury it somewhere.?'

'No no..., on the Tuesday morning of 9/11, before I made my way over to Manhattan, I put her body in the chest freezer in the basement. The intention was to get rid of it later, but at the time, because of the media attention I had brought upon myself I didn't get the opportunity to move it.'

'So when did you move it?'

'I didn't..., it's still in the chest freezer in the basement, up at the house. She's been there all those years, but that's not your concern right now. Anyway she's got company these days...'

'Are you going to kill me as well, is that why you drugged me, is this poison going to kill me?'

Ross moved closer to Eve, put his hand in his shirt pocket and produced a small white card, shoving it into her face.

'Read it, you fucking whore, read it out loud!'

'What is it?'

'It's your obituary, now read the fucking words out loud!'

Eve tried to move her body, but she was helpless, she looked at the words printed on the card and screamed, the last two lines lingering in her brain.

'Read it Bitch!! I want you to read the fucking words!'

Eve cried and her lips trembled as she read the lines,

> *This Gemini Was Adaptable*
> *An Adventurous Lover*
> *She Was The Life Of the Party*
> *But Got Caught Out Under Cover*
> *Now The Ghost Will Oversee*
> *Her Final Curtain Call*
> *But It's Always A Good Day*
> *When Geminis Fall*

Ross picked up the baseball bat and struck Eve's jawline perfectly, you could hear the lower jaw crack as her head slumped back against the couch.

She was in great pain and her head was spinning. Eve was

struggling to speak coherently but she had to ask the questions. 'You're him aren't you, you're Silas, you're the ghost! You're the one that has been killing all those women.'

'Yes Eve,' he whispered in her ear, 'I'm Silas, *I'm* the ghost! An appropriate name don't you think? For the past five months I've been invisible, wandering around the City of New York, stalking my victims, flirting with them, then bringing them back to the house where they died, with no link to me whatsoever.'

Now I'm on the brink of achieving notoriety, and I have you to thank for it.'

'How am I to thank for all of this.?'

'Don't you get it Eve? you're the instigator of all this, I will be forever known as Silas, the serial killer, the ghost of New York. The ghost that appeared in the night and disappeared back into the darkness, never to be seen again and for the second time in almost twenty years, a Gemini will have fallen. Tomorrow morning when your body is found, this card will be attached to it, you will be just another victim of the ghost, Silas will have killed again before he disappears for the last time!'

'But why Ross, why did you have to kill those women, why did they have to be victims of our marriage?'

'The answer is very simple Eve, the dead women and myself included, are victims of your infidelity, if you hadn't been fucking around those women would still be alive!'

'But how, why did you pick those women, police reports said that the killer knew his victims, how did you know them?' she asked, finding it more and more difficult to move her lower jaw.

'That was easy, I made sure that every **ameRKomm** employee's computer was hooked up to the main server, I was able to trawl through the social media history of all our female employees, their friends and their friends friends, I had access to tens of thousands of women's timelines. It was so easy to select my victims, by February I knew the birth dates of over twenty thousand single women living in New York City alone, I just simply picked women three to four links away from the employee's timeline so that there was no real connection to anyone in the company. Each of the five victims were the only child of its parents marriage, they had no siblings, no brothers, sisters, it meant that there would be less pressure on the cops to pursue the murders. Take my third victim, my Pisces selection, Charlotte Hoffman, can you believe there were sixty four other selected girls for that star sign, I wrote all their names on pieces of paper, rolled them up into little balls and put them in a hat. I looked into the hat and all the balls were screaming, "Pick me," "Pick me," "Pick me." After I gave the hat a little twirl, it was Charlotte who was screaming the loudest, so I picked her! – Isn't that fascinating!!?'

'If you remember, after 9/11, because of my heroics on the Hudson River, I was asked to attend a lot of the memorial services across the city, say a few words to lift the spirits of the people. I used to talk about Rebecca and Michelle and how the loss of the twins affected my life, but unknown to the congregations that were listening, I wasn't talking about the twin sisters, I was talking about the twin towers and how I managed to use the whole situation to my advantage. Every time I finished a sermon and walked back to my seat, I could see the people crying, people wanting to shake my hand, people just wanting to touch me I would always whisper those words to myself,

"But it's always a good day …
When Geminis fall"

'YOU'RE INSANE … DELUSIONAL … EVIL … YOU WON'T GET AWAY WITH THIS!' screamed Eve.

'And then of course there was Natalie's father, Geoff…, and her ex husband Troy, they both had to die as well.'

What!!? No, no!! That's fucking crazy!! I don't believe you! Geoff committed suicide, everybody knows that he couldn't live without Michelle, even Natalie accepted that, you're making it up, I don't believe you' shouted Eve while spitting blood and tooth fragments onto the floor.

'Why would you want to kill Geoff? He was a good husband, a good father, surely, even you must acknowledge that!'

'Yes, he was all of that, but…, he had something on me, and I knew there was no way he was going to stay quiet. I couldn't take the chance!'

Ross placed the bat on the table and sat down, he was on a roll, he hadn't planned it, but he was on a roll, he was going to tell her everything and he was loving it!

'Yes, Geoff was a likeable guy and his death was unfortunate, but he had to die, his death ensured I would have everything, the company, the money and the power, he died so that I could marry you, do you see where I'm going with this Eve, they all died because of you!'

'You said Geoff had something on you, what was so bad that you had to kill him?,

'It was a couple of weeks after 9/11, Geoff and I were summoned downtown to make statements, we both travelled to police headquarters together in Geoff's four wheel drive. Along with making statements, we were also asked to provide hair brushes and toothbrushes belonging to both Michelle and Rebecca for DNA testing.

In what should have been a formality, Geoff and I both made and signed off on statements, confirming we had both been talking to our wives when the South Tower was hit, I actually broke down and cried as I signed the finished statement, I was pleased with that, it was a good performance I thought.'

The cop recognised who I was and asked me for a signed autograph, so he could give it to his son.'

'So why did you have to kill him?' Eve asked.

'On the way back to the house, Geoff had been very quiet, too quiet, so I asked him if he was okay.'

He pulled in by the sidewalk, turned off the ignition, and asked why I had lied, why had I given a false statement to the police when the last person I had a conversation with was his wife Michelle, not Rebecca, you see I didn't know that Michelle hadn't switched off her phone, and Geoff, well…, he had heard everything said between both of us, about you, about the divorce, everything, in fact he was convinced that Rebecca wasn't even in the Tower building when it was hit. I had to react quickly, I had to make up something and I did. I told him that I had made the statement to protect the twins and I would explain everything when we got to the house. He wasn't happy with that, wanted to know more, so I told him that I had information that could implicate both of them in a financial scandal, that I had the proof in the safe at home.

Once we arrived at the house I offered him a drink and added the toxin, similar to what I have just given you...'

'So you drugged him as well!?' said Eve, spitting more blood and tooth fragments from her mouth onto the carpet.

'What happened next?'

'When it got dark, I put him in the 4 x 4 and drove back to his house, I parked the car in the garage and put him in the drivers seat. It was simple after that, I attached one end of a hose to the exhaust and stuck the other end through one of the cars air conditioning vents.

I made sure that the garage was air-tight and switched on the ignition. That was it really, neat and tidy. I had rectified the only flaw in an otherwise flawless operation.'

'So all those years that Natalie has struggled, trying to come to terms with the fact that her father committed suicide, always questioning why he never left a note for her, why he never said goodbye to his daughter, it was you who killed him! You heartless fuck!'

'What about Troy, why did you kill him, why did he have to die?'

'It was Troy who put Danny in the hospital, he beat him senseless to the point of nearly killing him, for the safety of Natalie and Josh he had to go, I did the world a favour when I did him!'

'And what did you do with his body?'

'Ooh..., you're going to love this...,' Ross said, now getting overly excited about the whole thing. 'He's also in the chest freezer in the basement up at the house, he's keeping Rebecca company as we speak, maybe I should turn the basement into a crypt, maybe have my own personal mortuary!'

'YOU'RE FUCKING INSANE ROSS, ABSOLUTELY RAVING FUCKING MAD, YOU KNOW THAT...!!?' Eve shouted at him 'But..., I don't believe you Ross, it's a pack of lies, I think you have made the whole thing up, calling yourself Silas, craving for attention again, trying to tell me that Rebecca has been in a freezer for eighteen years and now you tell me that Troy's body is in the freezer as well.

'You're a fucking nut job Ross, it's laughable what you've just told me, you've made the whole thing up!'

Ross could feel the veins on his temple expand, Eve was making fun of him, taunting him just like Rebecca did all those years ago and he wasn't having it.

'*YOU THINK I'M LYING!!?*' shouted Ross, his tone now more menacing than ever.

'You think I'm making all this up, well I'll prove it to you, bitch! I'll prove it right now, let's you and I go for a drive, out to the house, we'll go down to the basement and we can look in the freezer together, then we will see who's fucking crazy!'

'I know you're lying, Ross, if you had done even half of what you claim to have done, you would have been caught on camera footage somewhere, in one of the bars, a car park, a street. You would have been picked up on camera somewhere, even just once, it would have been impossible to remain undetected all the time, nobody could be that lucky!'

'But I wasn't lucky Eve, luck had nothing to do with it, you forget what ame**RK**omm's industry is. We manufacture sophisticated electronic equipment for many markets, the CCTV industry being one of them.'

Ross got up and walked across to one of the desk drawers by the TV and pulled out a little electronic switch, no bigger than a postage stamp and pointed it at Eve.

'See this little beauty Eve, it's called a shutter stick. What it does is, it temporally shuts down the CCTV system of the shop, the bar, the restaurant that you are in, before you enter the premises you just press the button and it disables the cameras recording system for the duration of your visit, you can drink your beer or eat your burger without anybody watching over you, basically you are putting "Big Brother" to sleep while you do whatever you want in privacy. When you leave the premises, you just press the button again, "Big Brother" awakes from its slumber and the world carries on. Nobody will know that their system has been down, nobody will be the wiser.'

Ross looked at his reflection in the mirror hanging on the far wall, the tormented rage had not receded, he could see that the veins on each side of his forehead were still throbbing, Eve had provoked him into a rage, he knew he would have to calm down, take a breather, he picked up his glass, poured himself another bourbon and sat on the chair across from Eve,

'By this time tomorrow Eve, after your body is found, the cops will come calling to my door, they will gently break the bad... the sad news that you have been the latest victim of Silas the Ghost.

I will be asked to identify your body, and, although obviously under duress, I will give such a wonderful convincing performance, the people of New York will grieve for me, they will weep for me, their American hero, widowed for the second time, again under tragic circumstances.

In a week or two I will have you cremated, your ashes scattered along the Hudson, the public will be told that this is what you would have wanted. In the meantime, Silas will have disappeared as quickly as he had come to be, the Ghost of New York will be exorcised and the jigsaw of the Zodiac will be complete!'

39

Ross strapped the adhesive tape across Eve's mouth.

'Time to go Eve,' he said, as he picked her up, tossed her over his shoulder and headed for the elevator. Each apartment in the block had its own private elevator which descended to the car park located on the basement floor.

Once he had reached the basement, he clicked the shutter stick, disabling the apartment block's CCTV, put Eve in the trunk of her car and headed for his Shangri-La on Hyland Boulevard.

As he drove along Jefferson Boulevard, Ross could hear the sirens wailing behind him in the distance but he was unable to tell whether they were police, fire or paramedics. Since he was travelling in the direction of the county hospital, he convinced himself that it was paramedics reacting to an emergency call, however, as he looked in the rear view mirror, he could see the two police cars speeding up behind him, the blue and red lights flashing, the sirens wailing.

Ross froze as the unmarked cars caught up alongside him, and for one fleeting moment he thought that the game was up, but in a flash they had gone past, overtaking him as they proceeded through the red lights, continuing to travel down Collingwood Avenue at breakneck speed.

'Fuck..., that was close,' he thought, although he knew he had nothing to worry about, he was confident that he was always one step ahead of the law, his meticulous planning of all the murders guaranteed that, it was flawless, they hadn't christened him "The Ghost" for nothing, there was no evidence, no clues left behind, the cops had nothing to go on, and after tonight, it would become another unsolved murder, another cold case gathering dust on a shelf in some police precinct downtown.

Unlike the others, he hadn't planned on taking Eve to the house, he was going to dispose of her body, taking her directly from the apartment to the already selected wooded area close by. He knew it was against his better judgement, he knew what he was doing was a calculated risk, but she had touched a nerve and he would prove to her, he had to prove to her beyond doubt, that he was Silas, that he was the Ghost of New York.

40

Natalie Johnson was busy in the kitchen, putting the finishing touches to the three tier birthday cake. She was pushing in the last of the birthday candles when the doorbell rang. She opened the front door and was surprised to see Max Hammond standing on the steps outside.

'Ah, detective Hammond, you must be here about Danny, can you do me a favour before we start, will you get the cars moved around to the back of the house and come in by the back door, I'll explain everything later.' Max met Natalie at the rear of the house and they both walked along the garden path.

'How is Danny? Max asked, 'I hear he's recovering well!'

'Yeah, he's doing fine, he's out of the wheelchair, walking with the support of crutches, his doctor's say he'll be out of the rehab centre and back home with us in another two weeks, Professor Nielson expects him to make a full recovery. Have you got some information for me detective, have you found the guy who beat him up?'

'Well, what happened to Danny is not exactly why I—'

Before Max could finish what he had to say, little Josh ran out to the garden shouting, 'Mummy quick! Hurry!' and Natalie ran towards her son while shouting at Max,

'Come on Inspector, you're going to love this!!'

Ross Kingsley got out of Eve's car, went to the trunk and pulled her limp body up onto his shoulders.

'*I'll show the bitch!*' he muttered to himself as he opened the front doors and stepped inside. The interior lighting in the hallway flicked on and as he kicked open the main doors of the living room, he could hear the voices start to sing.

'*SURPRISE!!* Happy Birthday to yo—'

Ross Kingsley stopped and stared in disbelief, his body froze.

In the room, there was a large gathering of people, all wearing party hats, some setting off party poppers and streamers, balloons were dangling from the ceiling above his head and it was then he saw the multi-coloured message that was draped across the wall on the far side of the room.

It read happy fiftieth Birthday Ross, our great "American Hero."

People who had just been singing, started to scream, others just looked on in horror as Ross Kingsley dumped his wife's unconscious body on the marble floor before fleeing out the front door, hurtling down the steps, racing back to Eve's car.

The fucking bitch! The fucking bitch tricked me, she knew there was a surprise party here today, she walked me right into it!'

As he sped back down the drive heading for the opening black gates ahead of him, all he could hear were sirens that were getting louder and louder. 'Where the fuck is that noise coming from?' he was shouting to himself.

There was nothing Brad Donovan could have done, he tried his best to avoid the red coupe that had driven onto the main road from out of nowhere. Ladder 43 ploughed straight into the car, crushing it against the ten foot stone wall, the car exploding into flames on impact.

Because of the intensity of the fire and the overbearing heat, Brad and his team were powerless to help Ross Kingsley, he was pinned in, trapped, unable to move his body, he could only move his head, ironically, just like his victims before they had died.

Ross screamed in agony as the flames engulfed the car, by the time the firehoses had doused and put out the flames completely, only a blackened corpse was all that remained in the driver's seat.

41

'So come on Sherlock, don't keep us in suspense, we know you can't wait to tell us, just how did you figure out that Ross Kingsley was our serial killer, our Ghost?' asked Sharon.

Max look around at the people gathered in the room. Pete, Sharon, Brad, the professor and of course the Chief of Police, big Philip McKenzie who had kindly invited himself to the house, fully aware that the press and the cameras would be arriving shortly. Max slipped his hands into his trouser pockets, sat back against the wooden table and began to speak.

'Last Monday afternoon, I called to a car dealership just north of Queens. The showroom Manager informed me that they had sold in the region of fifty of that series model since the start of January 2019, I asked him for a printout of all the buyer's names, and the dates they were bought, which he duly obliged. I took the printout back to the car, and studied the list of buyers. Obviously I was only interested in the January purchases because our killer first struck in January when he murdered Wendy Carlisle, but not to arouse the showroom manager's inquisitive nature, I requested the total sales for the year to date.'

'Clever detective work Max,' said McKenzie, who was wearing a smile as wide as the Hudson River itself.

'There were eighteen of those model types sold in January, of which fourteen were sold before January 20th. As I read down through the list of January buyers, I froze, my heart almost stopped! Guess what the sixth name down on the list was?'

'It was obviously Ross Kingsley yeah' snapped McKenzie, feeling good in himself that he was the first to get in with the answer.

'No Chief, it wasn't, to be honest, if it had been Ross Kingsley's name on the printout, I might not have put two and two together, it was in fact his companies name, ame**RK**omm, that caught my eye.

The company had bought the car on January 5th.

The moment I read that, I was blown away, in over five months other than the video from the fish tackle shop, we had nothing, not a single clue and all of a sudden, out of the blue we had our first real connection with Wendy Carlisle's murderer!'

'But how?'asked McKenzie, 'Wendy Carlisle was involved in real estate, she had no link, no connection to ame**RK**omm…'

'You're right Chief, she hadn't, but her close friend Susan Carter had!'

'Sometimes I am a little disrespectful to DNA and forensic science, I've always said, that above all else, you go with your gut feeling, as a cop it was always this something that steered me in the right direction. Yesterday, having read the printout, it wasn't just a gut feeling, it was much more than that, the knot in my stomach was been ripped open, at last, I felt we had something to go on!'

'So what did you do next?' asked Sharon.

'I gave Susan Carter a call, asked her if I could pop over to her workplace, talk to her for a couple of minutes just to clear up a few things in relation to her friend's death.'

'So on Wednesday, with my head still spinning, I walked into the ame**RK**omm building and took the elevator to the twenty first floor. Once there, a young lady was kind enough to put me in the direction of Susan's office and I had a brief conversation with her. I enquired how she was, how she was fitting back into the ordinary daily routine of life and brought her up to speed on the ongoing investigations, the usual stuff. 'However to be honest, and without appearing to be cold towards Susan's ordeal, my being there had nothing to do with her or Wendy, I just wanted to case the joint, suss out what went on there, get a feel for the place, use it as an opportunity to talk to a few of the other employees.'

'When I had finished speaking with Susan, I stepped outside her office door, and just as I turned to say goodbye, someone just brushed past me and for some reason which I can't really explain, this eerie feeling came over me, like as if a spirit of some sort had just passed right through me, as if someone had just walked across my grave!'

'The hairs stood rigid all the way down the nape of my neck and as I turned to look, to see what had just happened, there he was... "Silas", the Ghost of New York was standing with his back to me, walking towards the office straight across the hall.'

'But how did you know it was him if his back was turned to you, you couldn't see his face, how could you have possibly identified him?,' Sharon asked.

Max looked at her and smiled,

'Remember when you and I spent the day at your house, sifting through the evidence, looking, searching for a breakthrough? What was the last thing we looked at that day?'

'The camera footage from the fishing tackle shop...?' said Sharon, not sure whether she was asking or answering the question.

'Correct!' said Max.

'But having gone and looked at the images of Wendy and her killer in the car park, there was nothing, absolutely nothing to suggest that Kingsley was our Ghost!' Sharon said.

'Correct again!' said Max, 'not at the time no, but let's watch it again.'

Max nodded his head, Pete pressed the play button and the people in the room watched the recording in silence. With the exception of Max, all eyes were now focused on the screen.

When the recording had finished, Sharon shook her head from side to side, unsure at what she was looking at.

'I'm sorry,' she said, 'but am I the only one in the room who doesn't get it?'

McKenzie was also looking a bit perplexed.

'Me neither', said McKenzie, 'I didn't see anything that would have suggested Kingsley was our man.'

'I didn't expect you to,' answered Max, 'I didn't expect any of you to, because... you weren't looking for it.'

With the exception of Pete and himself, it was clearly obvious that the captive audience were just as baffled now as they had been minutes earlier.

'Pete, put in the other disc!'

This time they were looking at a recording of the evacuation of Manhattan on the morning of Tuesday 9/11/2001, just less than two hours after the terrorist attacks on the United States of America.

A couple of minutes into the recorded footage, the camera focused in on Ross Kingsley as he shepherded terrified New Yorkers aboard his boat, a couple of minutes later, the cameras again focus in on Kingsley as he jumps into the Hudson River, to rescue an old woman from drowning.

Max slowly walked over to the recording machine, pressing down on the stop button.

'Now this is where it gets interesting,' he said,

Pete and I are going to press play simultaneously on both machines, thanks to our techno genius Adam, from the IT gang over in Brooklyn, he has managed to interface the two recordings, which will now come up on the same screen, side by side, on the left hand side of the screen, the news cameras focus in on Ross Kingsley as he climbs from the water back onto the boat.'

'In full glare of the world's media and its cameras, he performs a simple habitual exercise, a habit that he probably carries out many times during the day, every day, without even realising that he does it, on the right hand side of the screen we will watch our suspect walk across the Bootlegger's bar car lot with Wendy Carlisle and as he does so, he carries out the very same ritual as they walk towards his car.'

Max presses the play button and for the next couple of minutes on one half of the screen, they watch Ross Kingsley on his boat, putting his hands upwards to straighten his tie, not once, not twice, but three times as he stares into the worlds cameras.

The left hand side of the screen which is playing simultaneously, shows Wendy Carlisle walking towards the car with her killer as he raises his hands to his neck, fiddling with what appeared to be his tie.

'Holy Sweet Jesus!' roared McKenzie as he watched the recordings in tandem.

Although the recordings from the car park did not give a full frontal view, there was no doubt that it was the same person carrying out the same ritual on each screen.

'When I stepped outside Susan's office last Wednesday, although the suspect had his back to me, his hands were fidgeting with something close to his neck, he was fidgeting with his shirt or his tie, and it was then his behavioural patterns clicked with me, behavioural patterns that were consistent with Idiosyncrasy!'

'What the fuck is that...?' asked McKenzie.

'It means to have a peculiar pattern of behaviour or thought, it's like you can do something many times a day, over and over, and you don't even realise you're doing it. Kingsley had it and it proved to be his downfall. I knew then we had our man, but I needed hard proof if we were going to nail him.

After leaving the building, I went straight to the 9/11 archive library and watched old footage of Kingsley saving so many lives, I couldn't believe that this was the same guy who was now killing those innocent women, women that he had handpicked to commit those heinous crimes.

'So why didn't you arrest him there and then?' asked McKenzie.

'I didn't have to' replied Max, 'We were still in the Taurus phase of the Zodiac, it would be another five days before we passed into the Gemini phase. I knew I had a timeframe available in which I could exploit to keep him under surveillance, Kingsley wouldn't be doing anything until then and given that he usually preyed on his victims at the weekend, we were looking at Friday 24th/Saturday 25th of May at the earliest!'

'For the past couple of days, Pete and I had been following Kingsley around, monitoring his daily routine, Pete kept tabs on him during the day and I being the nocturnal creature that I am, observed his movements under the cover of darkness. During those couple of days there was nothing out of the ordinary to report as Kingsley went to work early in the morning, returned to his apartment in the evening and going by when all lights went out in the apartment, Kingsley was in bed before midnight practically every night of the working week.

This morning, Pete took over the stakeout and I headed home, had a few beers, went to bed and slept for a couple of hours. The only thing was, for those couple of hours that I slept, something was hitting against the inside of my head, like a woodpecker nesting on a branch, pecking non-stop at the trunk of a tree, it went on for what seemed forever. Eventually I got up, made some coffee and began browsing through some notes that I had been sorting through for the past couple of nights.

As it turned out, the last notes I had looked at before I finished my shift, was the first interview with Susan Carter. I had no reason not to believe her statement, but something was not right, not all the boxes had been ticked, something was missing and after the second cup of coffee I knew what it was and I rang Susan's mobile.'

'What was it, what was missing?' asked McKenzie.

'Be patient Chief!' quipped Sharon. 'You know he doesn't like to be interrupted when he's on a roll!'

'Between everything that was going on at the time, I failed to ask her a simple but relevant question!'

'And what question was that?' asked McKenzie, instantly realising that he should have kept his mouth shut.

'I never asked her, who her boss was!?

'During her interview, Susan told us that the reason she did not turn up on the evening in question was because her boss had told her she was not to leave until a client query was sorted. This morning she told me her boss was Ross Kingsley and she always reported directly to him. Unknown to Susan, he had deliberately kept her back in the office, it was part of his plan, Kingsley knew that when he turned up at the bar that evening, Wendy would be alone.

'But if you had asked the question, if you had known that Kingsley was her boss, would it have made a difference? would the circumstances have changed?' asked Sharon, trying to assure Max that he was not to blame for Kingsley's evil acts.

'Right now I don't know,' answered Max, 'and to be honest I don't want to know, I'd prefer to think that because I asked the question this morning, we got a result, we nailed the bastard!

'How did you know he would strike today? and how did you know his next intended victim was his wife? asked McKenzie.

'During my conversation with Susan earlier this morning, she told me that she was looking forward to going to a surprise birthday later in the evening. She told me that Kingsley was fifty today and his wife was throwing a surprise bash for family, close friends and some company employees at his place.'

'So Kingsley himself was a Gemini!' said Sharon.

'Yes he was' answered Max in an upbeat tone, the motherfucker was a Gemini himself, the fucking irony of it!'

'Pete and I set up our surveillance post close to the apartment block from 2pm and waited. A couple of hours earlier, Pete had secured the search warrant for the apartment, so we had everything in place if we needed to act fast. Pete covered the East exit and I covered the West exit.

There wasn't much activity going on, a couple of people going in and out, a few cars entering and exiting the underground car park, but nothing that would suggest there was a party going on.'

'By four thirty, I was getting a bit worried so I rang Susan's mobile,'

'Hello detective, asked Susan, 'what can I do for you?'

'Susan, you told me there was a party going on this afternoon for your boss, exactly what time does it start?'

'Oh, it's already started Detective, we're just waiting for the boss and his wife to arrive.'

'What do you mean you're waiting for them to arrive? He hasn't gone anywhere! From what we can tell, he's still in his apartment and his car is still in the car park!'

'Well, maybe Eve is driving, and she's going to get some surprise as well!'

'Why do you say that?'

'Well, it's Eve's birthday on Monday so there's a double birthday celebration going on, looks like it's going to be a long night!' laughed Susan.

'Susan…, where's the party happening? asked Max who was now starting to worry a little.

'Same place I told you earlier detective, at the Kingsley residence.'

'You mean the apartment, yeah?'

'Oh no detective, the apartment would be too small for this crowd, the party is at the main family residence on Hyland Boulevard, we're all out here on Staten Island!'

Max dropped the mobile onto his lap and began to shake, the sudden rush of blood to his head making his body come out in a sweat.

He composed himself before picking up the radio.

'Pete, are you there?

Pete…! Pete…!! *pick up for fucks sake!!'*

'Yes boss, what's up?'

'Why didn't you pick up?'

'I just left the car for two minutes, got myself a coke and a burger from the food hall, what's up?'

'We're at the wrong fucking address!! get the sirens on and put the foot down, we're heading for Hyland Boulevard, whatever happens next, we need to make sure we take this guy alive!!'

'When did you find this out?' asked Pete.

'I just spoke to Susan, the party is at Kingsley's house, not the apartment, and if I'm correct, his next victim is going to be his wife, I just hope we're not too fucking late!'

'And that was it really, you all know what happened next, his wife was the main target in all of this, the other girls were just pawns in the game that went on in his evil and demented mind, plus the fact that we have uncovered two more bodies from the freezer which brings the total death tally to eight.'

'Eight that we know about!' added McKenzie.

'True' answered Max, but from what his wife Eve has managed to tell us, I would be surprised if there were more bodies hidden somewhere. Kingsley wanted to tell his wife everything, she was going to die anyway, it was like he wanted to confess to all the murders, he wanted it off his chest before he stopped his killing spree and who better to confess to but his final victim, knowing she would take his confession to the grave. It was a clever plan, in fact it would have been pure genius if he had pulled it off.

'But Kingsley underestimated his wife, Eve knew she was going to die, but she was smart, she knew there was a surprise party going on back at the house, she had organised it with Natalie weeks earlier and she knew there would be a lot of people at the house, she somehow had to persuade him that she did not believe his story, that she was not convinced he was telling the truth so she worked on his ego, she goaded him into bringing her back here, telling him that he was delusional, calling him a liar, a cheat. She knew if she convinced him to take her to the house to prove that he was telling the truth, there was a good chance that she would survive, and she did, it saved her life!

There are just a few things to wrap up in this case, Herb is gone to the hospital with Eve. He's on duty there until Pete and I get there in the morning.

The doctor's say that Eve should be okay to make a full statement sometime tomorrow.'

'Chief, I think you'll be the most qualified to handle the press, so the rest of us don't have to worry about getting our mugshots on tomorrow's rag sheets. At the moment, there's a gaggle of them gathering at the main gate.'

'Yes, I noticed that,' acknowledged the Chief.

'I think it's fair to say that we have had a successful conclusion to our serial killings, unfortunately, the fact that "Silas" is dead, takes some of the gloss off our success. It would have been nice if we had squeezed a confession from him, see him dragged through the courts before rotting away in a maximum security prison for the rest of his life, however, we can be thankful, "The Ghost" has been exorcised for good, the families can now grieve for their loved ones and the women of New York can sleep easily again.'

'Until the next one,' said Sharon.

'Until the next what?' asked McKenzie.

'Our next serial killer, our next Ghost.' answered Sharon,

'Perhaps he's out there right now, walking the streets, stalking his first victim, carefully choosing the type of woman that he wants to kill, someone who looks like his mother, his ex-wife, his ex-girlfriend, or perhaps someone who just simply happens to be a brunette called Charlotte.

Max could see McKenzie was not going to be deterred by Sharon's predictions for the future, he was beaming from ear to ear, unable to contain his delight in the knowledge that he would once again be in the limelight, the flashing lights, the cameras, the extraordinary case and its narrative making all the front pages. For all his years on the force, this was the highlight, the pinnacle of his long career, if there was ever an opportune time to take up the offer of a pension package, it was now.

'As for you Brad,' said Max, 'you're the first fire fighter I know that started a fire and couldn't put it out.'

'I wasn't even supposed to be working tonight,' answered Brad, 'I was filling in for one of the lads back at the fire house, he and his wife are expecting their first baby, so I agreed to do a couple of shifts for him. However tonight has prompted me into doing something that I have been deliberating for some time, I'm going to hand in my resignation, I've seen a lot of bad things over the years, including 9/11 and I've had enough, it's time to go home, spend some quality time with my family.'

Max beckoned Sharon to one side. 'Sharon, I need you to do something for me, you're the only person that I can think of that will handle this situation in a caring and understanding manner. Natalie is upstairs resting, she's in deep shock and certainly too distressed to be interviewed by anybody at this time. There's a police psychologist on the way to speak with her but before she arrives, I want you to go upstairs and talk to her, explain to her how her father died, tell her that it was her godfather, her uncle who failed her and not her father. Although she still grieves, I'm sure she'll find solace in the fact that her father did not leave her on her own by choice. With Danny coming home soon, I'm sure she and Josh will be okay.'

'Okay Max, I'll do it right away.'

'Thanks Sharon, thanks for everything,' said Max as he kissed her on the cheek, 'I think I'll slip away while the going is good, let McKenzie take centre stage for the cameras.

'What about you Max, will you be okay?'

'You know me Sharon, I'll be just fine, I'm off now to treat myself to a nice cool beer, I've started to take a personal interest in this Zodiac shit so maybe I'll check out my horoscope, see what's in store for me tomorrow!'

As Max left the house, Sharon followed him out onto the driveway.

'Max…, remember the question I asked you a couple of weeks back, about what option would you have chosen as punishment for our killer…'

'Yeah, vaguely, why…?'

'I know the answer.'

'How could you? I didn't give you one!'

'No, you didn't Max, not then, but you gave me the answer tonight.'

'And how did I manage to do that?'

'Earlier this evening as Ross Kingsley found himself pinned in, his body crushed in the blazing inferno of his wife's car, screaming in agony, unable to move, unable to escape the burning fuel, the searing blistering heat that was devouring his flesh all the way through to the bone, I glanced across at you Max, I looked at your face, and the answer was written all over it.

Max said nothing, he just looked at her and smiled.

He knew she was right, Sharon was always right, but he would just never admit it.

'I've been thinking,' said Sharon, fluttering her eyelids, a devilish smile enhancing her already beautiful face.

'Why don't you call to the house tonight, we could order in some Chinese, have a nice glass of wine…'

'I don't know if that would be the right thing to do Sharon, considering our past history…'

'Max, for the past six months, we have worked very closely

together, this case has proven that nothing is impossible, plus … we make a good team, I think we deserve another shot at finding happiness together.

I'll be wearing my green boots…' purred Sharon.

'Red or White?' Max asked.

'Why don't you choose Max, you seem to know your colours pretty good!' retorted Sharon.

'Green it is then, I mean *white*! … fuck, I mean white' said Max smiling, as he relaxed back into his seat and drove out through the gates of the ghostly Shangri-La.